I0782150

SCREWDRIVER

Screwdriver

Ian Bloom

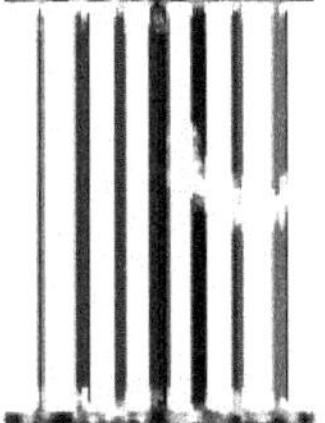

IAN BLOOM

Ian Bloom is an American art dealer and founder of Natural Gallery.

SCREWDRIVER

"F1 teams need a driver who will consistently set lap times that are 100 percent on the edge"

- Jean Alesi

"We must not be deprived of this spectacle"

- Jean Baudrillard

"Ambition is a dream with a V8 engine"

- Elvis Presley

SNAKING BENDS made the drive swell. The curves seemed to sway the lights as the auto carved the path, with the sight of road through the windshield just a suggestion. A guideline.

Speed had made the line seem solid through to the ocean. Air, feel, tonic, different by the salt waters. Breathing here should have been constant. Had Jean Barry been able to at all times at all places, it would be the first choice.

1

The Ford Falcon floated idle at the traffic light. Yellow, then red, now green. Jean Barry did not mind, but after his second pull on the smoke, it was about time. Then, the Falcon flashed hazard lights and lingered on a left blinker. Drift motion to a clearing. The Driver had to be the Guy.

"Hel's the name. Hel Lambert."

"Howdy." Hel lit Jean's cigarette, made eye contact.

"Now, I'm saying this plain and simple."

"Hel, just spill it. It's not your job to make it simple."

"Rollie said you're a straight shooter. Okay, now, there's all these people gonna be after me."

"How you say?"

"About three o'clock last Sunday, this haughty junkie comes onto my lot. I sell used cars, beauties, classic shapes. Sure, he's a dapper guy, a Euro three-piece, some jewels, and a Stetson hat. But, he's a junkie. Trust me on that. And he keeps tapping his finger on the hood of this Chevy I got out front, and then he keeps looking around, surveying the field, like he's shook up by invisible watchmen, when he says he has cash and he wants to trade his ride for a better one. Now, I'm all ears—cash transaction is the best transaction. Of course, he had a desirable ride, one of those '84 Jags, XJ, black, still had that jet cockpit vibe on the inside."

Hel was a Polonius reincarnate. Get to the point and quit the verbal blitzkrieg. Jean lit another smoke. Patience squeezed at his gut. He considered. So, a standard scenario. Shady character, shady intent, and a caustic lackey caught in potential crossfire. Jean preferred to pass on involvement in this one, but Hel Lambert urged three thousand through a grip of hundreds. A professional is a professional. He took the bat. And thus, Jean went to drink.

Randolph's was his swanky retreat, lots of wood, tinted by shady bulbs the bare minimum for reading, heritage Americano types and auxiliary nymphs longing for the past in all but wardrobe and phone habit. The strain of a phonograph emitting only jazz. In the backroom, old timers occupied the best seats and the rest were left empty. It was fear or respect, or both, probably nothing. Here, Jean sat. They all smoked outside. His credit was flawless and by dint of his naturally calm demeanor, Jean warmed the lost bartenders' hearts. He considered himself a keen drunk, any commotion never resulted in damage to the property. And by default, his gait added to the ambience. Jean sipped, smoked, stared. Conducted preliminary research on his mobile device. Some red flags slipped to the digital surface. This was expected.

Twelve months ago:
Vice Squad busts sex ring at used car lot.

Seven months ago:
Circus tiger on the loose. Baboons on the lot.

Three months ago:
Local rapper Yung Cheeseburger buys six American classics, calls next single "Hel's Motor Angel."

One month ago:
Shark Studios sells BURNING RUBBER stunt cars, auctioned off at Hel's.

Reported news was quite exotic, thought Jean. Operational prowess was never his prerogative though he figured it best to arm himself for the day's mystery. He'd eat a cheeseburger. *Burning Rubber* received righteous reviews, and a sleepy desire to cruise toward the Perrault Theater gained momentum, the spectator's fix growing. A throat hairball caught Jean's windpipe off guard and made him excrete a yellow yack by the side alley. *Should have switched to non-methols when I still had willpower*, Jean noted. The liquid membrane settled and crackled dry against the neutral sunrays. Prosaic summer daze in paradise. A blank stare did not take in cultural desolation, cars passing, cigarettes littering, consumption constant. *Why in God's name did I still take up the racket? I could have run a maid service, traded stocks, or just quite, no use. Can't let that heat burn me down.* Jean's mind steadied.

His craft was hitched on the precipice where Bad Guys pushed other Bad Guys into social oblivion. From a distance, they all looked like heroes, or martyrs. *Nihilists.* Either way, it made no difference.

Jean had a thing for mirrors. They did not hide the plight of conscience. They accepted the display and did not lie. He could not say the same for himself. Another hairball.

Reverbed back into the bar, Jean erased his broodings. Never healthy to be self-analytical; poison, the way his inner monologue spewed its filth. The laconic bartender Luke slid Jean a whiskey spiked with bitter orange juice. Eggs over easy beckoned Jean to a corner seat. The seagulls bellowed by the terrace. Nearing high noon, the time of day when the slugs baked on the blanket of sand and were seasoned with the salt waters.

He left his Lanvin sports coat on the seat. Caught a floating melody through the cool breeze of opulent perfume and silk curtained bosoms and behinds. Once at the terrazzo, his vision froze. That damn Minerva bracelet, true mark of a siren. Harley, Harley, Harley, the kind that always escapes. A vicious player who made the game play by her marks. Blue-chip prospect, once-in-a-lifetime talent, intently seemed to throw it all away. Satisfied with a fleet of trusted patrons, boy-toys footing her bills. Jean had had a good time their first meet, and she had made it clear he could again, or so he kept telling himself.

But when it came to the beat, Harley was a "*he's your guy*," except he was a she, and she was the measuring stick for the standard. She pecked the Cincinnati kids and elicited a Marilyn smile-gasp, then curved her stilts to the counter. Tapped her finger, snapped with a whoosh, and Luke went to work on her special mojito.

Indirect awareness. Peripheral contact.

"Where's mine?"

A pause.

She Vogue-posed her profile and glanced down the counter. A light fixture glimmered in her pupil. Jean smirked, held a groan inside. He slid the cigarettes over, and she caught them with precision. Fire to her dying butt.

"Now, what's the word that got you staring so far?"

No response. Jean would not cave so easy to Harley. She was still the feline, and she could wait. Luke brought her the mojito. She turned her Corvette of a body to face Jean, the creases more prominent with her leaning posture.

"Hey, straight shooter. Don't be so coy. I thought we were just business."

"Don't be so quick to judge," Jean said, letting it go. She smiled sultry and gazed voilà, kicking back a sip.

"Well, you're awfully partial to listening, so I'll go first, Jeanny."

"Floor's yours."

"My man, Valeri, just returned from Montreux, ran into a player of interest, Brubaker, you remember, that Brubaker of Brubaker & Sons quasi-hedge fund capital market cashier, heir to some sort of board room throne, the one that beat up his actress girlfriend and then saddled up to be a Delta pilot, just because he could—so this Brubaker tells Val that he's starting up his own airline, has this fleet tip-top tuned and sprung for aerial action. An IPO in six months, guaranteed, or call him a schemer about to make off. Looking for venture capital. To get to my point, even though that last part is a striking contradiction, I have a meeting with this guy tomorrow, just for an overview, no dotted lines to be signed or nothing."

"I'll see what I can find, and if I see something, I'm your guy."

"You're always my guy."

Throat croaked up. Of course she knew. Tied him up in a wordplay vise.

"Sheesh, I can't seem to remember that Brubaker's girlfriend by name, sure her face was an icon, hell, Jean why didn't you say so?"

"You love when there are chains to tug."

"She was quite a catch. Definitely as far as couples go, you two were a superb match. Your colors complemented one another. Now, be a hero and tell me her name."

"Vittoria Vitti."

"Vicky Vitti-Vitti. Vitti, Vitti, Vitti. How did I forget that name? Name has poise."

"Look, Harley, best to cut the act before these guys realize your lady's skin shed full-off, and now, you're just a slim built Gorgon chimera."

"Chimera's three creatures, rude boy."

"Use your imagination, smokey."

Jean had an open window to tap out. This broad could battle for days. Harley's voice sobered up, and Jean departed through the arched doorway.

"Hey, Jeanny B. Best you call up Miss Vitti. Have a feeling she needs someone special in her life right now!" Ignition, fire, smoke, Dion and the Belmonts, and skid out to the road. To Jean's chagrin, the radio dispatched a ball buster. Home run distance out the first game of the doubleheader, broke the news, interrupting "Runaround Sue."—Apparently, Echo Park was invaded by California condors, all 300 of them endangered behemoths inexplicable and miraculous to see and hear as loquacious Bobby Bravo announced the happenings on KRBC.

Times wreaked a foreboding scent of smut. The toilet bowls had less water in them on account of the two year drought and the ever drying reservoir supplies. Coupled with the rising costs of utilities relative to bonds, REITs, and all the typical fixed income streams, the flushes were shallower. Less suction into the vacuum of tubes that spiraled into the void of sewers. Hence, there was more residue, shit resin, piss orifices, on fifty million public toilets in the greater Los Angeles area, and thus, the times reeked of smut. Thank God for cleaning supplies.

Jean caught the scent at the most dangerous interchange in America, 405 dash 101. It stank. Only contributed to the danger. All the sewage cascaded into this vortex and lurched about in flux between uneven ground, dried up drain alleys, and the incessant labyrinth of pavement and circling tires. The set piece at the reservoir dam, invisible decay catching the air and firing it into all those traffic ridden noses. All the military base scenes in *Escape from New York* had been shot at the dam. No wonder Lee Van Cleef had such a flummoxed disposition. Radio waves tuning back in, to the road, to the driving function.

Jean really wanted that cheeseburger.

2

JEAN GOT to where he was going. Whereabouts Reseda Boulevard and Vanowen Street. Middle country suburbs. In-between places where time neither carried forward nor traversed backward. Lots of mini-malls and billboards not on freeways. This particular stop was on a side street called Sleepy Hollow. It was a cul-de-sac, the type of dead end where kids played in the street and did not disrupt the peace because it was a street going nowhere. Point being, this was a house contracted out for the pornographic cinema. Some palm trees, a cobblestoned walkway, and a complementary fountain with cupid and his compadres.

Yung Cheeseburger greeted Jean at the door, customary since the days of New York State pillage. In a yesteryear, a past reality, partner enterprisers casually social networking, specializing in the social exchange only drugs could reduce to the lowest common denominator. In any case, they were here and now in the west. Yung Cheeseburger perceived himself a rebellious social skipper, general of an army with no concrete direction but a strong opinion, someone to usurp the systems in power via an open trade with what financiers coined "cultural charitable contributions." This was purely mutual, and lucky for Jean, Cheese happened to be involved in a smorgasbord of relative associations.

His new nickname, or alias, whatever he credited himself with was now Charles Mosskey. Jean couldn't explain. He knew the true Cheese name, Leo Dmitri, was only a start and a middle, the end unknown, and therefore, possessing of the liberal doubter's benefit.

"Barry, you twisted rebel, so glad for you to come. What's up, my mane?" Fists friendly. "Why, come in, come in, let me reveal my craft to the supreme justice incarnate."

Mosskey had a predisposition for edgy energy exchange, an insatiable survival drive to kick-start Jean into a productive monetary position. It did not faze Jean because he assumed Mosskey's intentions were righteous, of a purely egotistical nature, the id unbound. The interior was only a place that could reveal some conduit of a half-hashed innovative movement Mosskey declared mythological realism. Curious intellectual attraction between the two of them. Jean entered.

The inside of this crib was marked by Doric columns, headless busts on half-Doric columns, and Getty-thieved vases depicting insipid lores of mythologies long lost in the pop cultural lexicon. In the foyer, a wide loaded ensemble, regal from afar, caught Jean's eye. The faceplate showcased the birth of Achilles. Jean followed the body baptized in holy water minus the heel. Where Thetis should have been holding the heel, a scorpion snatched, and under the water, Achilles suckled a three-dimensional nipple. Subversion understated the superficial. The surrounding space consisted of various harlots vegetating in real time. Mosskey rescued Jean from his visual masturbations. Freed from the overloaded circus, Jean focused on the porch, Roor and joint accompanied, all thanks to the gracious Mosskey.

"The only times you make an appearance, nowadays, you're either seeking a jolt to the heart or a ruckus for your dick. But this is certainly just fine."

"Barry, don't you question my judgment. You may be a rotting scoundrel full of philosophical lore and whimsical jargon, but you always find yourself not even an arms-length away from my loud grin and Nordic sneer. Now, smoke your damn given loads before I tell you something you should know."

Mosskey felt stress. Jean possessed luck. When Mosskey stressed, Jean learned the most about things, things as in specifics, about him, about her, and about all the rest—and all the rest was Jean's target. Mosskey began a rant about the social spectacle, the nebulous takeover holding our time space continuum :

"At the technological level*, when images chosen and constructed by SOMEONE ELSE have everywhere become the individual's principal connection to the world he formerly observed for himself, it has certainly not been forgotten that these images can tolerate anything and everything. Because within the same image all things can be juxtaposed with contradiction."

Mosskey volleyed his wayward whims for all ears, standing erect, illumined by the sun's transferred window waves and rays, as if he was a demigod in a cartoon outlined by Hercules. He was lost in this old scrap of papers, and when the first page fell to the floor by Jean's foot, Jean glanced to see what it was—some Situationist French revolutionary banter. Jean allowed Mosskey's attention, but noted it had more to do with the orator than the writer.

"Nowadays, when I get on this sativa, my mind just races. It's the primary mode to imbue creative faculties to my work."

Simultaneous processes. Through the reflection of the hallway in the window, Jean stared at a bulbous behind. So rotund, it might as well have had its own satellite. A fly buzzed on the window, too, on the ass, and Jean wondered if this observation signified Mosskey's primal portents. Vapors and airs permeated the foreground.

"I stick to books."

"Mane, you gotta see past the past, mane. The future, dude, my phone has a fingerprint scanner. It's 1984 like George said, but only the positives."

"No. With your Debord Situationist stuff, all those images spoon-fed to sculpt the mind's eye, you follow, then reading is the only thing that can give you access to the wealth of the human condition, any insight prior to the spectacle."

"Hey. There was always a spectacle. Just now, everyone's in on it."

"No escape."

"Certain. Check out this new fire beat Attila Hung made for me. He's my new diamond sprung from the rough, producer cut in Aphex Twin's vein, pseudo-hybrid Scott Storch and Benedek except with Slim Dunkin's bravado."

All ears. Stress dissipated in its entirety upon the luminous descent into auditory medieval dungeons. A whiny organ, faint in the background, functioned as the bass to set up the dirge mood, the beats per minute winding up and up and unwinding back down while the second set of keys made it a hit waiting to be struck.

After the last funk-infused synth solo, Mosskey cut the sound off and turned his face toward Jean's contact vision via the mirror on the adjacent wall. Mosskey snickered. Jean nodded his cap in accord.

Should be a banger if preparation and tastes coincide. Jean had doubts though hoped for the best for his comrade. Simultaneous processes. The separate rooms of the house vibrated with gasps, wallows, and guffaws in discordant waves by lad and wench. Jean sensed opportunity emerging for new discovery. Mosskey handed Jean a business card, a new client with wholesome funds. The client contracted Mosskey's production services big time and could assist in some puzzle solving. Jean gave Mosskey the last menthol cigarette, and it was a healthy exchange.

In the car, Jean inspected the card.

Dynamo Properties, Inc.
5225 Wilshire Blvd. Suite 777

●

Across the bottom of the card was a black circle, a black hole perhaps.

Smoke lit, engine revved to function, and then a loud bang penetrated the cabin. On the other side of the bang was a healthy knock of a fist, a fist on the arm of a flimsy plank of a girl. Could not have weighed more than 100 pounds. Heels that made her seem menacing from the seated vantage point. Jean thought she was a starving quarterback. Her facial expressions showed wrinkles and dripping black mascara that only drips from tears. Her pouty clouds kaleidoscoped through retinas and no chance in hell could Jean ignore her help-seeking gaze.

Window rolled down. Immediately, she hit the unlock button and planted down into shotgun. Jean felt swindled by yet another siren. Listen below the belt and accept the consequences.

Her name was Monica, and she had a meltdown. She said Jean looked different than the usual suspects and saw him as her only hope. Some innocent unholy thoughts spewed into Jean's head space. She said in exchange for getting her gone and gone fast and now, she'd buy the cheeseburger. Jean reiterated this was his first priority. Some gentleman.

At or about the 405-101 crossing, Jean slurped the last of the chocolate shake from the In-N-Out Burger. There, Monica cooled her jets, and intrigue spouted from her unholy lips.

She was a friend of Vittoria's, had been in the same acting class, and claimed she had met him once before when he and Vittoria were still a thing. This once before had been at the Washington Club off Sunset. On account that everywhere in that vicinity was black out land, Jean could neither confirm nor verify. He gave her doubt's benefit. She seemed to know the minimal share of credible personal information, including some mention that Jean had been wearing a Raymond Weil watch of regal style. Jean's father's watch, so she was right, he guessed. She told him her porn track had been spurred by some sort of blacklisting because she did too many drugs with the late Art Matheau right around the time he remade *Spawn* into a Hollywood blockbuster, won an Oscar, and overdosed on stage while receiving the trophy. At which time, she froze in the audience, mortified and lucid to a runaway point, attempting a stage run to come to Art's aid. The end result : her fainting, the trophy decapitated, and the Academy embarrassed and all of it on display.

Now, porn was her path but she only did girl-on-girl or threesomes or orgies. She was never boinked. Didn't really bother Jean. He let her dissipate her inner whims on noise-canceled ears, and as they emerged from the Sepulveda Pass, the Getty Center shone luminescent as the sun entered its descent to Kingdom Come.

If a woman believes you're a good listener, she'll tell you anything. In fact, she will volunteer, if you catch her at the right wrong moment, and this felt rightly wrong. The clock said a quarter past seven, and Jean figured this whole deal required more probing.

3

JEAN WOKE up on the couch. His face felt groggy and red stained his tie. Red wine, he guessed. Monica's heels were poking him in the ribs. The door to his bedroom was closed, and the cabernet bottle lay sideways, the cork nowhere in sight. Jean's head spun, and to gather his senses, he smoked a cigarette. By the lighter on the coffee table, his wallet hovered, the card poking out of the fold. He slid the card out, stared at the black hole, and remembered why he called it a black hole. The night before, he had decided to treat it as such because it made him feel it was a portal, an odyssey to the inevitable netherworld. Jean held the card up to the eastern sun sharking through the bay window and unexpectedly viewed through the translucent backside.

There were markings. The backside showed a drunken rendering of Jean's personal font, reasons inexplicable. Cabot House, noon, today. Important*. With an asterisk.

Maybe she'd know. In the meantime, Jean made coffee and rebooted his mind into functioning with the **Journal**. Typical shit headlines, as in remarking and benchmarking the progress of the typical companies, governments, and big players inclusive, updating the reader of their debating and proposing to initiate courses of action and implementations that very well could trickle down to an endpoint affecting the reader's existence as a member of America, Incorporated. But, no, hey, Jean corrected his id—one headline in the Money section reeled him in.

*Government defense contractors set
to expire, rumors of dark horse candidate
for the subsidies.*

Before he got ahead of himself, as was his tendency, Jean volleyed to a shower to massage his thoughts. He was gladdened to find a fresh roach to augment his lavatory experience. When he got out, roasted afresh, Monica had already tidied up the place and posed, twirling her hair. She stared at the orchards in the yard when a loud smash pop of bubblegum broke Jean's concentration in enjoying her backside. With a grunt, Jean rumbled and poured her a hot mug. She looked beautiful in the morning.

Jean kidded her about all the trouble they had gotten into with the fun the night before, and in ten minutes, they were set. Jean dropped her off some place he was not going to ever find her. He had that noon lunch to go to for whatever reason he had not figured out.

The Cabot House was a post-Ivy League social club that had imploded into a feng shui, seedy Chateau Marmont crossed with the veneer of a private bake sale at any gourmet supermarket that specialized in organic products and complicated vitamin combinations and extracts. The Art Deco exo-skeleton suffocated under the weight of metal stands and screws to hold plastic screens purveying the daily televisual blotter. If only one could still smoke inside, it might not have been half as morbid.

Jean perched in a corner booth. The maître d' assumed Jean was meeting someone and had his name on a reservation for four. Displeasure. Regardless, a little rush was natural. When it finally hit him, the last words Monica had said as they had parted ways: "Say hi to Rex."

Rex was a mutual acquaintance. Jean had only made the connection that Rex was an associate he and Monica shared the night before in the bloodbath of liquor consumption and smoke and mirrors, and to be expected, they both knew him via Vittoria. He ran a few books for the races and had a racket in Elysian Park with a few seniors that was known to have been quite profitable during the recession. Thereby, the racket had skipped multiple levels to go bicoastal, launch online, and legalize means to launder all the monopoly money. All the shakey money sifted through sweat-stained fingers, mucked up keyboards, rusting circuit boards, and corrupted digital synergies, substituting hands until it all ended up in his. Case in point, Rex was now an independent film producer with a hairy chest, balls like a bull in heat, and money to spend. But he needed a script.

Monica was always a sweet spot of Rex's, and she had put them in phone contact the previous night. They had gathered that he had a pitch for an idea for the concept of a plot that could be constructed into a script that could catapult him to the A-list of the industry and attract supreme talent, if only all signatures and documents were signed and Jean would agree to consult for accurate measure during the course of production.

Shit, Jean said silently, *I've got five minutes to bullshit a sellable idea to preclude my next agenda—Rex was in serious cahoots with Brubaker himself.* What a blend Jean had in store.

Rex lurched to the table accompanied by two Polish editorial models with friendly smiles and two-faced stares. Pearly white teeth sure seemed coke ridden. They refrained from ordering any food. Rex demanded a kielbasa and an omelette spiked with rum. Gnarly toro. Top notch, onto business. Reiterated his passion and credibility with noted affiliations that no one cares about unless addicted to social media and *Variety* or *The Hollywood Reporter*. Smut salt, the girls wanted to see what a real Hollywood pitch and sell or pitch and catch sounded like, and he had brought them along. Dgaf.

So here it went.

"Think *The Big Sleep* meets *Trainspotting*. It takes place in Los Angeles. The sleuth is hired by an aging hotel magnate to: Rescue his daughter from the clutches of her skag-addicted college cohort, determine if she is criminally liable, serve justice, settle the mishap, and reap the rewards. The mishap is murder, by the book, at first, but the junkies acquire an exorbitant amount of heroin by Misfortune masked as Fortune. Then the smugglers of the heroin show 'belongs to' looming large over a group of innocence-parched youth. In a nutshell, the surreal sequences of drug use circa *Trainspotting* superimposed onto a Los Angeles beachside palette, a slow-speed car chase, no, not chase, a car spying, some sex, and then a *Die Hard*-esque, key on -esque, thriller climax in a hotel owned by the magnate. She, the rightful heir. By the end, she's using the private dick to play decoy to the smugglers, take blame, cover up her crimes, and it's too late because he's already fallen for her, and as far as ending, the dick can either be left high or dry or both, but I always prefer happy endings, like at the end of *Wild at Heart*. You be the judge."

Rex sipped his mimosa, stared down, removed his Oliver Peoples eyeglasses, and stared up. A rickety smile crossed his face with dimples on top of dimples and grease marks newly shining in accord with his greaseball hair. Sold was an

understated assessment. The blank chicks were excited, present in the company of decision makers of such magnitude. Possibility.

He went on a hyper-business diatribe about the four quadrant money coordinates and how this could only increase the exponential potential profitability of the film while allowing him to maintain artistic integrity. Rex and Jean toasted, and Jean could tell he was in for a drawn out occasion. Rex declared Jean had a familiar face, and after the Monica via Vittoria double whammy, they became definite buddies. They shared honest laughs about the Monica-at-the-Oscars fiasco, and Rex promised this to be her comeback to clear the Walls of Jericho, to open the gates for her industry participation. Eventually, Jean put on an act that the drinks were too early too fast too many and had to get going after the final one.

Rex begged Jean to remain. Jean said after this one, this was it. Then, Jean casually remarked how is Vittoria going with that guy, Brubaker, his name, and the beartrap abstractedly self-armed with decadent cheese. Rex invited Jean for a night on the town with him and Brubaker a couple clock turns. Guaranteed excessive swell times. Last sip and on his way, but not before Rex could share: Vittoria disappeared the day after she and Brubaker were with him at The Tux. No one knew her whereabouts.

4

THE ADDRESS: 5225 Wilshire Boulevard, Miracle Mile. A self-loathing namesake. The foreground housed a large construction site with remnants of smelters now defunct but yet to be demolished. Rebar, cement trucks, and orange helmets looked ominous in the smoky sun as Jean approached Dynamo headquarters. The elevator was broken so he took the stairs.

Another Art Deco type, except this was the real thing. On the fourth floor, Jean peeked down the old elevator shaft, one of those with the metal sliding gate like in a warehouse loft or a Golden Age flick. The entire seventh floor was Dynamo, Suite 777. Some sick joke. To avoid the runaround, Jean loaded his palm with Rex's business card and the black hole card Mosskey had given him.

The waiting area was staunchly dormant, no secretary. Just closed doors translucent like a marble orb of quantum energies. The walls were bare except for deft camera placements, nodes conspicuous yet decorative, centered in wooden panels where antique paintings should have been. On the table were neither magazines nor journals, only a speaker box that reminded Jean of the one the angels talked through to Charlie. The speaker box hummed alive. Jean had a cigarette held on his lip, about to light.

He didn't.

"Prospective client, if I am correct?"

Jean's body language was amicable, and the doors buzzed open. He entered. The hallway had deep mahogany wood floors. His steps echoed down the way. At the end of the hall was a dame of majestic height and proportion with the satin gloves and a vintage Chanel suit, he guessed. She motioned Jean to the leftmost door at a dead end hexagon overlooking the construction site across the street.

Jean gathered his senses in a clearly lit, auburn carpeted room, absent of life. She pressed a red button on the wall and complementary cigarettes, a perpetually flaming ember, and an array of liqueurs were unveiled upward on the table. Jean made himself comfortable and did not take a look around. It was obvious that the environment was so intriguing that his peripheral senses told the whole story. This was all facade, and only human contact had a chance to direct him to any substance.

The office had all the makings and arrangement of an executive suite for a particular individual, a boss figure of authority, yet what it seemingly lacked was a series of family photographs, a degree or two, or an arbitrary stack of work papers. No personalized phone. Eerie forebodings. Jean sipped his scotch slowly, and the rocks dissolved.

The worker pumpkins across the way marched as a troop conducts reconnaissance or a sneak attack slash ambush in a guerrilla warfare escapade. The silence broke when he heard running water.

Jean peered out of the room into the wood paneled hallway. Another door opened diagonally from where he stood. The liquid sound streamed briskly at a constant speed. Jean slid across the hall to view a Venetian fountain with angelic, demigod-like figures. He smiled. It was not the least bit grotesque. The new viewing room had a Zen aura with the fountain and a pure aromatic scent, but behind the fountain lay a boardroom table worthy of accommodating forty-year-old fortune keepers. On closer inspection, each seat had a microphone attachment on the left armrest and a fold-out keyboard where the table would be like on a first class airplane seat. There were enveloped narrow slits on the table where each seat was aligned, and Jean snooped about, clicked a button situated by some knobs and other buttons under the frame, and a screen volleyed upward out of the slit. High tech stuff, Jean considered. The screen came to light with the negative image of the business card. Guess it was not a black hole at HQ.

Since Jean had much experience journeying in places without permission, his senses numbed, no rush elicited from the occasional trespass. He grew bored yet assumed there was more that could meet his five senses in artifice. He heard steps in the hallway and sauntered toward their sounds. By the time he returned to prime viewing position, only a sliver of a shadow broke the floor and it went one way: right at the hexagon portal.

He followed lightly, no tension, and both doors right at the hexagon were open. He chose rightmost right random to come into a stone room. Could have been a tomb had he woken up there without seeing how he had entered. Instead, Jean saw it was a mausoleum of sorts, housing massive circuit boards and servers beneath stony trenched protection. Must keep the electricity cool. *Absurd*, thought Jean, *the upfront or sunk cost had one intent: mystery maintenance for aesthetic pleasure.*

The room through the other right way was where he should have gone when he had seen the shadow. Here was a mirror image of the first office room, literally situated opposite in every respect, even amber frame and liqueur arrangement composed on the table. A snippety old man in a turtleneck, velvet sort coat, breathed with a slight buzz. Name was Cameron Gödel, had a menacing handshake, sculptor's hands, bushy eyebrows, and a hearty mug sinewy with wrinkles and bronzed skin. His gaze reminded Jean of Steve McQueen, if he had had Laurence Olivier's superficial disposition. When Gödel put on his spectacles to focus a look at Jean, he looked more like a philosopher or magi from the Ottoman Empire, so Jean imagined. Simple and plain, this guy could have had a bust of himself, and Jean could not look down or funny at him for it. Jean trusted his gut and introduced himself, honest-like.

"Name's Jean Barry."

"Sense your tour has been a tad incomplete. Pleasure to meet and to inform you as best I can. We, here, at Dynamo, prefer to be as brief as possible in client interaction."

"Like in the shadows."

Gödel offered Jean a smoke. He declined, for the present. Did not want to appear nervous. Gödel continued.

"If you possess a card, it means you have been referred by a current client, or a past client. Regardless, that is a necessity for our discretion."

Jean played his game of words. "Don't seem to handle any typical properties at this joint, am I right?"

"Sales to the public market are not publicized, by Dynamo."

"This must be quite the racket, secrets and keys to doors that are always closed."

"Haha, Mr. Barry, I can assure you it is quite more than the current and the waves on the surface. Now, you seem a witty sort whose time has enormous value, so I'll get to the point." He handed Jean a brochure and said, "Follow along." The first content page had the motto, which Gödel recited like a true tradesman, orator, or political attaché.

"To maintain and guard information as stewards of property." The following page had a languorous definition of property. Despite the excess, Gödel's sermon-like charisma drew Jean into focus.

"'Property,' defined as anything that is an attribute, quality, or characteristic of something. In this case, some**thing** is some**one**, a what or thing that is some unknown and is meant to be wielded to be unknown, or utilized in any fashion the client sees fit.

"We have a three-pronged approach," said Gödel, "and three departments to coordinate the three-pronged approach in cohesive order, thereby reducing systematic risk." He motioned for Jean to approve the pitch so he could carry on, or to pause if Jean had any questions. Jean motioned for pause and did his best to conceal a smile.

At this juncture, Gödel extended his left arm towards the door and lithely present was a stoic fellow, bearded, gangly, and clothed in denim from his head to his leather toes. His name was Randolph, Todd Randolph. Mean moustache on this chap. He had paint marks on his jeans, but they looked natural, not machine spilled.

He unveiled a digital display projection with the click of a handheld contraption and shone illuminated was a negative of Da Vinci's "Vitruvian Man." "The body as a commodity. The body is an entity that can be utilized for reward. In the framework of capitalistic hegemony. . ."

Jean stopped paying attention and adjusted his visual lens so he could look at Gödel and Randolph from a wide angle. They looked like extras in the movies, the bit players that made the pictures come together to make superficial sense. That is, to pull off a semblance of reality. Jean caught back on, ". . . if the body is an entity, de facto, it can be labeled a corporation, and thus, lifestyle can be governed by the treatment of the corporation in the context of law, and societies and governments, as in, if the individual adheres to the treatment a corporation receives in respect to law, and perceptual social mores or bases or biases, he or she can maximize his potential earnings potential and ubiquitous fulfillment of life's goals in a carefully constructed time span. Whether that encompasses the illusory possession of power or the creation of monetary wealth, treating oneself as a corporation will nevertheless commodify all resources. Assets become myriad, ad infinitum, via the variability governed by the definition of an asset, and we have not even touched upon the class of an asset."

This was all a bit overwhelming. Too much for Jean, yet Todd had held Jean's focus with the trite logic of his monologue accompanied by visual dots easy to connect. The "Vitruvian Man" had morphed into an animated body, placed in a series of uniforms, performing functions, climbing ladders, rising in rank, and benefitting from physical function as a body. This could have been shown to third graders, and they would get the gist of it. And English theory students could argue for days about what the speech entailed in respect to the image. Both men stood at adjacent ends of the table and waited for Jean's cue. Jean cued them.

"Provide me with an example if that's possible."

Unfortunately, they could not, or rather, would not. They seemed to be testing Jean out for worth, or merit, or something substituting for hoards of disposable cash.

Jean asked about their service limitations. They answered tongue and cheek with a few chuckles that that was not a concern applicable to their business.

The charade was waning, and Jean began to ignore his own intent and present motive, thoughts of more base responsibilities like what was the meal he'd consume later that evening or the intrigue of an imminent encounter with Harley were rising in priority. The smooth bite of the drink in hand lapsed into his daydream, and the picture formulated rapidly upon their unified statement on the word "leverage." Right then and there, this confirmed bullshit.

Jean came out straight with them and divulged false information regarding a client presumed theirs. Jean thought he was wrong, but his profession comped just enough clout to remain relevant to their fixations, and they referred Jean to one of their upstanding operatives called Dohltrey. Jean kept beating around the bush about what information he possessed that could be of use, and based on the men's sales pitch slash mirrored curtain, Jean's wits seemed to falter. He took the cigarette finally.

Waiting for a final word, the men appeared cold and calculating, like shaded eyes at a poker table, but not in the least bit menacing or ready to jump across the table and into fisticuffs. They were office men with civility and for once—Jean thought this a good thing.

"Look, I don't really see any future between us."—And with that, Jean retracted to whence he came, yet they suddenly grew partial to sharing.

Randolph spoke, "Why, good man, don't be so quick to judge. You should not be surprised, we're all in-house, and our reach is vast, to put it starkly."

Jean needed some fresh air, and he got some on the junipered terrace only Dynamo had on this floor only. What the fuck was their racket, anyhow? Jean blistered internally. Some metaphysical baggage slammed his thought process, and thoughts returned to wagering the recent month's events. This could not be a simple front for a simple score—no drugs, prostitutes, laundering—no chump change. That speech had all the workings of something more valuable, the worldwide web had to be in play. The body as commodity. Got it, or good enough to get part of it. They were information traders, exchangers, brokers, and they had a lot of financial backing and close ties to closed doors. Heck, they

could be in on all Jean's rackets, and he couldn't prove it either way. But as long as Jean was still here, that word **"leverage"** seeped to the front of his mouth. He muttered it to himself. Hey, seize it now, what to seize, still unknown. Felt like one sorry rake.

The clouds got in the way of the sun and when it went shady, Jean went back inside.

The duo was where he had left them. They did their best to hide they were enjoying the tongue and cheek play they had coiled Jean into, engaged by information asymmetries, notes from Orpheus' underworld.

Be it as it was, Jean had nothing to offer except alignment in a loose legion, where if he found out anything, he'd pass on the information to them, and he'd trust they'd do the same. They let Jean chew off a piece of a bone as they escorted him out, but not openly.

The harlot secretary was the messenger at the door. "Mr. Barry, you forgot your brochure."

Tucked in was a note to meet at Satch's Diner off Tuskegee Road, tomorrow, noon, signed Luana. Guess she wanted out, or did she?

5

THAT ENTIRE episode tasted bitter in Jean's mouth, not the least bit sweet. Jean wanted some good meat so he went to Canter's, the best deli counter in the area and stopped off on Fairfax. Where all the skate shops and the janky stickers were on the street, Jean noticed a street graffiti area overrun with an obnoxious rendering of a black hole. Coincidence but a sure bothersome one.

When Jean got to where he was going, he sat across from Harley and did she have the dish. He could not help consider her get-up, a post red carpet bender. Her purse looked like it should have had a tape deck or just been a boombox minus the speakers on the sides. Jean stared. First, she pulled out an investors' report on Brubaker's; second, one on Dynamo Properties; and third, an oily extract of Afghan origin.

Jean said, "You, too?" in reference to the Dynamo brochure.

Harley went, "Like hell."

She refused to budge, and Jean let her in on some of the action, said she should accompany him to The Tux where he'd be meeting Rex and Brubaker, or if she'd like, she could already be there and casually link chains, the infamous run-in. Then she would see them under the influence to possibly gain deeper insight. Gut feeling, Jean explicated, was that it was not a buy and the ground floor was too shaky, on a shadow of a foundation. "Suit yourself, though. It's your money."

Harley laughed one of those knee jerking ones that makes the eardrum wince, just for effect. Not a bitch, just an asshole in a bitch's body. Out the window, on a billboard in the distance, Jean saw what he thought was another black hole icon, the exact one as on the Dynamo card and in the skater nightmare.

Harley saw him looking and stepped on his toe. "Whatever you are thinking, hun, you are probably right." She had that smug snicker still on her face, did not blink, looked at the billboard, then the Dynamo brochure, and then back at Jean. An All-Pro manipulator if Jean ever wanted to fornicate one. The rotten smell of corruption bequeathed her an allure and the scent of a woman covering something up. Anyway, she was in a stellar mood, due to his invitation to the Rex affair at The Tux, and spilled something contributory.

Dynamo was sprung headfirst from the aether as a shadow operation by Hollywood bigwigs who sought to control their stars and auxiliaries. To control the media's information overload, hence an underground sphere, anti-Internet, anti-paper, antimedia. The branch had gone to was the disinformation branch. Harley called it a "lesser evil" branch. Reason Dynamo was so vast and expansive was due to the capital reinvestment by all its clients, dubbed members. Technically all insiders, and as far as the very vocal ones, publicity generators, their managers ran the show. Insider trading was the practical pastime—if it was a father, then this Dynamo was the son. What got her involved was their ability to scour all trenches and pits of decay on all her boy interests. Likewise, she could control her reputation from straying from the straight-arrow line. Probably Mosskey was in on it.

Harley brought up the greater evil branch, the department of dissemination. Jean wanted none of it yet.

Either way, appraisers had estimated Brubaker's IPO close to $9 billion. This estimate was according to the meeting she had attended the other day. She had an offer on-the-table to purchase up to seven percent of the company's stock, not to mention options for an additional three percent, in separate one percent increments, and privileged shareholders' stock equivalent to bonds in riskless assessment. They both needed coffee, fast.

Jean thought, *with the NSA basically playing the part of Big Brother, credit Orwell, we must be in the station where the information black market ran rampant.*

"Is Dynamo American-based?"

"TBD. I'll find out."

Jean was not certain how to go about it, but Lambert certainly needed his professionalism to come into nature at the moment.

Off to the loo, messages checked, and the one and only was from Lambert. Awfully worried, decompensating based on his hissy auditory mimicry. About time, Jean should be learning some useful information, so he parted ways with Harley, and in the crack of a whip, she had multiple suitors connect gazes with her Black Mask eyes across the seating booth maze. The evening was misty fresh, as if the sprinklers had just showered the area and the concrete slabs shone luminous in the just-clicked-on city lights. Righteous time for a smoke. Jean figured to let Lambert sweat a little more—he'd still be rummaging around his seedy lot by the time Jean arrived.

A few moves ahead, Jean scouted operative Dohltrey. Had a mean mug, displayed via the digital search engine, some Sterling Hayden snout and jaw, a refined moustache. Funny thing though, was Dohltrey's digital association with a defunct zinc and diamond supplier. More digging, Jean discovered the company was considered defunct in that it had been smothered into a large conglomerate based out of Vienna for a tidy acquisition price just under 800 million pounds sterling. This was last year. Whatever his position was, it seemed to have authority based on his picture-perfect hat, overcoat, and the glare of a large-faced watch in the pixelated sunlight. The city light Jean smoked under went out, and it got shady.

Lambert was at the lot like Jean expected, and he sure had some sweet rides. Jean even asked if any of these cars went out for rentals—Lambert did not want to respond. He had more heavy issues weighing in on his pea-sized mind. That pea-sized mind sprung into a great oak when he showcased a newfound realism and substance on his personal account:

"Upon further analysis and reflection, Mr. Barry, I have decided to provide you with full disclosure regarding my case, and in-so-far as this absolute coverage can be of use to you, I believe it will necessitate any further involvement I may have on a person to person, face to face basis, henceforth."

"Uh-huh."

"You notice the sounds of airplanes landing and leaving. The point being, the airport seeks expansion—some new airline's coming in Buy, buying out all the old hangars, renovating them—they want more. See it, I got myself a most ideal-located property in this lot—standing in expansion's path. A massive target on my lot. Take it, as it is the one bordering the airport that is strictly commercial in operation and use. Now, you may wonder, just assume—I am a keen negotiator in the course of business and sought to truly delay any possible sale of the property, as my customer base has been extremely loyal and receptive to my location and dare I say, ambience, in the noted property. Quick aside, consider the Venetian blinds, the subtle placement of a gargoyle in each light post, and you could deduce I am a man of worldly tastes, not your run-of-the-mill sleaze-of-a-salesman. If I was going to be on the outs of this business, I would need as much guarantee as I could get."

"I'm waiting."

"—Don't get snippy, Barry. I'm on course to wire you another $3,000 tomorrow morning. See, what I have unwound is a delicate, potentially visceral scenario, involving me, the municipal powers that be, and the corporate powers that are coming into being—aka—the new airline. You see, they came in with an initial low-ball offer, masked as a fair market value of $15 million for the lot, plus transportation and storage costs for a six-month period following the sale—more like seizure, of the the property. I countered with $20 mil, eliminated the storage costs from the equation, and proposed a like kind exchange of property from a requested selection of their land holdings. They were surprised at my wit, no lobbying the next month. I did not cave though—I knew I was the dealbreaker for the expansion. Survey the land outside the north and south windows—the neighboring properties had been swooped up in that month of corporate absence. My hand was gaining precipitous momentum yet to be exercised, and I knew it, rather than feel pressured to retract to the initial offer. So, this takes us to August when a buffet of high-class escort types began to not only harass my premises but also to purchase more than a handful of sick rides. Let me show you the transaction records."

He did. Three Cadillacs, two Lincolns, and a sweet fiberglass 'Vette. Same could be said about the drivers, based on their license photos, imagining the rest of their features busted down. So, after the cars were purchased, an older lady came in; she went by the name Madame Bovary, twisted sort of dame allegedly, and she's busted by the Vice Squad on the property, and Lambert gets caught in collateral crossfire, damaged, still smitten with all the escorts. Things are too fishy for such coincidence. He thinks it's a scare tactic. Righteous tactic as it may have been, he still would not budge. He's out for blood, and when he declared that, Jean almost burst into a giggle. A half year passed by, then another incident poked its smut out of the crisis cracks when circus animals from a hangar across the street somehow escaped and ransacked the lot with coincidental malice.

Like Lambert said, despite the embarrassing spectacle, any media coverage was media coverage. Cover equaled more business, in his particular line of work. He did not defend his claim, but based on Jean's research, the claim of intent had certain support. Anyhow, the gist of the picture Jean could see was plain—machine driven intimidation, strong-arming Hel into selling. They had attempted light appeasement on the previous deal. Hel had stood steadfast. So now, Hel, harassed by loan shark types and the assorted ex-military security operatives, was scared as a ghost in a mansion too large for his desires. It did not help that his secretary had been distributing to the corporates the keen lead or tip on his whereabouts and motives and intentions. Siren.

The incident before the last (the last being the junkie transaction), a gangly group of swashbucklers turned up at his office and homestead, and he knew this because first, they had tied him up, then thrown him in the trunk of a sport utility vehicle, and taken him to his house and left him on the front lawn still tied up and wet from his own urine in view of his temporary kidnapping and humiliation at the defilement of his place of rest. These guys were easy to recognize, easy to spot, and they said they'd be watching—and we already knew for what purpose.

Jean recited his standard defense mechanisms to curb Hel's worries. "—Tread lightly . . . don't read too deep into things, but . . ." also, "I am not a bodyguard." —The sweat hanging under Hel's nose in a most morose light started to get on Jean's nerves so Jean told him to wash his face, collect himself, and get some rest. Jean was out of the door but before he could close it shut, Jean told him not to bother with the three grand due for tomorrow. Jean was not a bodyguard. Before Hel could beg or whine, Jean reiterated not to worry, that he would request more funds when needed, and then when Hel had more to share, he knew the proper channels for communication.

What Jean could not paint in the picture was the debonair junkie of the cash transaction. His file, in hand, was brief as words, absent of useful ones, and the name was certainly fake: Jon Dawson, but Jean called it in to a guy he knew for an alias checkup. Why the hell not? No photo, more mystery.

When he pulled up to the vicinity of Satch's Diner, Jean shot his eyes into focus and spotted the secretary waiting in a booth, alone. Upon further inspection he saw Dohltrey posted in a car across the way. Jean could play it two ways, and he decided to play it the second way, bypassing the booth exchange and the girl. With a blatant brake slam and a well-timed light of a cigarette, Jean reeled Dohltrey onto his tail and directed him to Lemming's a few blocks south. The coffee here was always better than Satch's.

The conversation was balanced, cordial. Dohltrey had cunning diction and a confident gait, especially noteworthy as he smoked a Nat Sherman. The prestige tobacco gave him a refined air and dignified his prolonged pulls and exhales. Relief sprang from Dohltrey's open disclosure, his lack of denial regarding anything about his affiliation with Dynamo. Judging by his dapper get-up, assumption was it was a custom-made ensemble cherry-topped by Ferragamo leathers, Jean considered Dohltrey notably compensated. Point of discussion, Dohltrey volunteered to be Jean's contact for any matters regarding Jean's probable contractual agreement with Dynamo, and it was Dohltrey's responsibility as agent to administer and perform his fiduciary duties to the best of his abilities. Since nothing was in writing, Jean considered it a sham.

The Santa Ana winds were coming in dry, and dust gathered on the blacktop by some trio of Dick Tracy types, footballers suited up to be gangsters. Dohltrey took no notice, and when he and Jean parted after a final smoke by the neon light, he still ignored them. When Jean left, two of the cars followed and the third went west the way Dohltrey went. Jean went south. A crow shit on his windshield so he got in the rightmost lane and parked in the nearest gas station to repair the damage. Birdshit was always a bad sign. The two cars were now in sight, and Dick Tracy filled his gas on the other side of the podium. Jean approached the passenger side of his car, lowered his head, and checked his teeth for flossable food. He could see the shadow of a gun holster in Dick Tracy's shoulder area as he uncorked the gas canister from his car. Jean crushed an empty pack of cigarettes and moved away from the car. In the mini mart, Jean purchased a snack. Out the window, he noticed Dick Tracy had gone along. Observation conjured a slight impatience, Jean's nerves specified, and so, reactionary, Jean consumed the ice cream sandwich, vanilla stuffed between two chocolate chip cookies. It hit the right spot.

Jean took a piss, too, and combed his hair. He had known this bathroom was clean. The few clouds that were there a moment ago had ceased to exist with the Santa Ana winds picking up pace. A plastic Coke bottle rotated over the bumps and cracks in the concrete and snapped into place down the curbside gutter. The television screen at the pump had rattled on and on about killings, the stock market surge of the day, and how an eight-year-old girl had been abducted, Amber Alert signals displaying on all throughways and freeways in the Southern California region. When Jean walked out to the gas pump, he remembered the blare of Jordan Delaney's prototype voice enunciating, "Rain in Death Valley. This message sponsored by Interzone Pharmaceuticals."

Back on the road ahead, Jean drove beneath the freeway overpass and—what had slipped his mind—came right back—that there was construction about this time in the evening; so he detoured to avoid traffic. The soggy layer of air distilled his visible plane. He did his best to be certain those Dick Tracy types kept invisible. Jean had a lot on his mind and did not seem any closer to penetrating conceptual axioms to come to any sort of understanding for his clientele.

Questions of worth: *Was I too soft for this line of work-now? No, like hell. Was I too tired? Maybe. Was I too indifferent to their outcomes?* Now, there was something to contemplate. Either way, Jean had inhibitions leave his train of thought when Dick Tracy Numero Dos pulled up driver's side, appeared amicable with a concerned innocent gaze, and levied Jean to pull aside by the public park ahead. Back mirrors were empty, there was only a couple parked cars on the right and none of them were Dick Tracy Numero Uno. Jean saw kids still at the park and decided to ignore the request. Instead, he highswung into fast gear and rocked ahead when the road got windy and upside the mountain. Okay it was a hill but it led to a steep pass. Still, low gears, engines revving—Dick Dos was keeping up, to Jean's certain dismay, and "Cowboys from Hell" pantomimed Jean's movements in an auditory sense over the radio's blare. Up the hill and through the canyon glut, they could be alone. Jean felt safety building force, collateral damage surface-level eliminated. Potential contact out of control.

The next song was just as fortuitous as "Cowboys from Hell" for the occasion, and Jean prolonged the fabrication of chase for thrills alone. Dos had a rising heart rate. Intensity on Sunset. An inch-close tailgate. Jean braked suddenly, rockers off stage, their cars touched behind and front bumpers, a slight dent on the fenders at angles, relational dystrophy, all dependent on whose car was the prime reference point, when Jean raced up Mandeville Canyon to go to a dead end.

At this point, the road was one line, winding, and there were no streetlights despite the sunset and impending darkness. Jean had dictated the arena. From the windows and curves, he saw another car close in behind Dick Tracy Dos, assumed it was Numero Uno. It was. They followed him up at a calm distance now because there was no escape.

Three and a half miles up, Jean pulled onto the dirt by a clearing where there were no properties within a football field's length in either direction up or down the road. When they pulled up, Jean already leaned against the car hood, stared into the abyss, smoked, and they came around to the front to disturb his line of vision. They had to have felt intrusive.

"What was that all about?" they asked.

"Had to be sure," Jean said.

"Sure of what?"

"That you were who I thought you were." They were not following his train of thought. Jean said he knew them, he had sent for them, but it had to look as if it was a pursuit, well, hell, not a trivial one, but one of high risk and potential danger. Jean underscored, "The watchers are out there."—These guys bought it on premium. Meathead goonies.

They thanked Jean for his insight, explained themselves as just following orders and that Jean needed to hear what they were sent to say as proxy for boss Gödel.

Taken aback, Jean pondered and waited for their recital.

Dick Tracy Dos was called Merv, but that did not really matter to Jean. What he had to say though, did matter, a great deal in the still clear canyon stopgap and the imminent interplay on the city marked by lights unseen.

"My boss, whom I represent, Mr. Gödel, instructed me to alert you of how you can be of use to Dynamo. In exchange for your services, Mr. Gödel and Dynamo, at large, are prepared to offer you a traveling correspondent position, or operations consultant, or head of security, depending on your performance in the matter at hand."

"Hold your horses. Are these your words, or his, verbatim?"

"A little of both. Hear me out."

"Enough with the formalities. Incentives are not the way to get me motivated or inclined to help you."

"Simple enough . . . well, Mr. Barry, the case of the matter is that Dohltrey is under suspicion of being in violation of corporate bylaws. In other words, we think he's a double operative—he's playing both sides—and with the sensitive information he has access to, we need confirmation and verification of the truth before we can take the necessary steps to resolve the security breach, if there is one."

Numero Uno said, "Cut the meat off the proposition's bones, you got what I mean?"

"Look, sleuth, you scratch our backs, and we'll scratch yours." All the information was in a folder they had handed Jean, and it was all surface level in substance, except for one striking detail that came in the form of a photograph showcasing Dohltrey with an expression of dismay standing next to a brazened wiry creature, inked all over, arms chest and shoulders, but no neck or hands. John Doe was in a wifebeater and a black '80s Jaguar was in the background of what appeared to be a wide open space with flat concrete ground. A runway.

6

THE INFORMATION oversaturated his consciousness. All these chips out of the woodwork had the same surefire voices, surefire phrases, and surefire deliveries of some semblance of the truth. What that was was relative and would never be more than that. The mix of experience lived was starting to simmer in his veins, and his capillaries, and an artery to his heart area was enervated by a somber pain. Jean was not even smoking. Just brooding, silent with the sounds of the tires, the pistons, and the shocks to break the wind's waning momentum.

At the red light at the end of Sunset Boulevard, the gas stations were empty and the waves were sleeping. The ocean looked boring. Jean liked the sight. No one else was coming behind so he stared and was pleased with the pause. It was never peace, resolute, absolute, into perpetuity. Because it'd all spin around the merry-go-round and repeat itself, the cyclical flush of the toilet, garbage in, garbage out.

Before the guy in a sport utility in the rearview could honk, Jean revved the engine forward with a light pedal kick. Back into the labyrinth . . .

The next morning, Jean was up and out early to check out the airports. The runways at Hope Runways by Hel's Lot did not match the photograph. Now, if they had had to, it would have all just been too easy. Some kind of a conspiracy. But, no, onward to LAX. There, Jean could not get a really good look at them all, but he had a gut feeling that would be fool's gold. Van Nuys did not check out, either. This photograph looked too quiet. He should have known. The mountains were much more akin to Burbank, and in his frustration at the waste of his first two reconnaissance hours, Jean consumed a large apple pie at a franchise deli. Casual bad call. Indigestion even after a smoke.

When he got to Burbank Airport, the sun was still low enough in the sky to wash the endless row of windows through Terminal A into white, blinding, almost sublime, were it not for the crimson red, no, cherry red, carpetway that followed the windows inside as the concrete slabs did the same outside. An immense parking lot for planes. Never saw any hangars visible from here, and after a walkaround, Jean was back to the beginning. In the dark, indifferent, and add to that, queasy. Jean felt there was a dump to be had in the next half hour, and in lieu of that, found himself at the sports bar in the middle section of the terminal watching a review on the Dodger Stadium condor phenomenon. Deep coverage. They had some guys from serious nature magazines, a few academic types with glasses and graying hair, and glorious athletes to comment on the explicable and make it sound plausible.

Even after two Irish coffees, the queasy feeling turned out to be a phantom dump, and Jean felt lucky because he had inspected the photograph with the white light from the rising sun augmenting his visual field. The license plate would be impossible to extract from the photograph, as would any easily identifiable landmarks of the Santa Susanna Mountains. One caveat to a negative outlook rekindled a positive sentiment. Via his portable atlas through his mobile telephone, and some meager deductions by his grand ego, the mountains in the photograph were indubitably enormous, gargantuan in respect to the ones displayed out of the Burbank Airport windows. Out of the vortex of information and life lived, Jean recalled visions of the time he had been a passenger in the Cheese-mobile on the north side of the Valley, had dropped acid, and had traversed the lowly foothills by Charles Manson's Spahn Ranch at the end of Topanga Canyon. Prediction was that this airfield was the testing grounds for the defense contractor Open Doors Technologies . . . cut the crap because he knew his hand could only reach so far.

Traffic shit on Jean and upon release eased him back to his office, deep sleep summarizing the daytime's remainder. It was kind of nice not having a secretary anymore, no wise cracks, or innuendos of flirtation, or a surprise coffee. Those little things lost to the efficacy of outsourcing administrative duties. The trade off was that Jean awoke past dinner-time and had to scurry home after the tobacco shop, and the liquor store for Fernet Branca and Kentucky bourbon whiskey for the flask for the night.

His place was sloppy, and the high-strung shriek of Harley coaxed him into movement as he spruced the place into some semblance of kept order. She wanted Jean to take her somewhere, guess on account of her challenges when it came to vehicular travel.

The Tux had an ornate level of artifice typically displayed within an amusement park, say Disneyland or Universal Studios, in that the flora and the fauna were hopelessly fake. It was natural immortality, and it looked appealing. It was thematically safari, reigning down a picturesque portrayal of the African Serengeti with bulbous acumen. The paradox, or just uncanny kick of the place, was that this could be experienced as leisure time, sans the air conditioning, the martinis, and the live music and clean water. Exoticism only exacerbated the pleasure centers, that is, as long as it was clean.

Another thing about this place was that the two adjacent drinking havens were associated by ownership with The Tux. Therefore, there was never a line or ruckus outside the front entrance. The idea struck

Jean as a stroke and maneuver of genius, how much more attractive a locale would be if the zombies and drunkards or an obnoxious crawly array of gold diggers was forever absent from the bowels of reality and could be framed in conversation as, *Remember all them? Why, this place is perfect because they're never there.* All in all, the start of the night had a seriously intriguing point of entry.

Upon entry the courtyard bespeckled with African influence contained a club in and of itself. Heck, Jean could have spent his whole night there and his satisfaction would have maximized at the halfway marker where there were vintage Land Rover Defenders accessorized as seating booths, with servers, not to mention the taxidermy work on the exhibited lions, lionesses, cheetahs, and even an assortment of elephants around the central "river-spa" fountain. The exhibited stuffed animals were arranged in such a way that you could view them in all their glory, within an arm's plus half length. But, instead of gates, or glass to serve as insurance, the motion sensors could detect if someone was approaching, getting too close, whereby the animal hinged to a hanger could be coaxed off to safety, whether it be back, up, down, or curved, as long as it was away. *Now, if only they could apply these motion sensors to cars, we would be getting somewhere,* Jean mused. In addition to the ground level ensemble, hanging from the ceiling, on all four walls and ceiling corners was an enclosed balcony, narrow in respect to the glass-bottomed enclosures that jutted out at the midpoints of the walls and united in the center in a herculean central orb, with a keen amber hue on the crystallized gloss bottom floor, so in a flurry of drinks, laughs, and out of focus peripheral vision, one could say it was always day-time in this decadent rut.

Further observation revealed the upstairs watcher's point as a shooting gallery. Guns had transformed into cameras in earnest farce. Nature was tame and vulnerable to the people, and thus, the ecological safari resulted in raucous banter promulgated by the neverending flashes of light beams hymning to the melodious bumrush of shutter and flash clicks. Jean was losing himself in the right side Land Rover Defender, the site of a most illustrious *menage à trois avec deux femmes et un homme.* You see, though, the man was a voyeur in that he commanded his place in the backseat with a cocktail in one hand, and a clove cigarette positioned on a long silver and black filter in the other. In all honesty, the *Mensch* looked too dainty to not be a Liberace influenced fairy. Not that there was anything wrong with that. But in his viewing arena were the two dames engaging in the most provocative of bum accentuating positional alterations, utilizing their silk gowns as flowing curtains that never quite revealed enough. From Jean's vantage point, this entertainment filtered through the front windshield simultaneously as the smoke caught on the glass and decorated the females' dynamics like the opening credits of a James Bond movie. Juxtaposed with the flashes from above, Jean was visually hooked when a courteous, classy hostess excused herself to Jean and led him to where he was expected.

At the end of the room were large, daunting, ironclad gates, and on the other side of them was Harley looking haughty and aghast at Jean's ditching her. She called it his disappearing act. Jean grinned and a whimper of a chuckle came out, but she did not hear it. Thank God. The next room was The Tux, what it was known for, and it had a Sahara themed quality. Not the Egyptian Sahara, but more the Algerian Sahara. Akin to Tatooine in the *Star Wars* saga. Sand blew under the glass floor to provide the visual sensation save the desirable touch. This place was privy to privacy. Harley and Jean lapped through a high-walled canyon corridor in the arena. Around one corner, Jean swore he witnessed Indiana Jones and Darth Vader sharing a joint. And around another pass, in a dimlit cave, were Tony Montana, Charlie Chaplin, and the third was either Austin Powers or Louis XIV. Jean could not make out what they were exactly doing, but it certainly involved divvying out paper money, piled neatly into stacks on the stump they were circling . . . . Harley said we were in, behind the lines, that these were employees taking breaks, off duty, before duty, after duty, or who knew why or when. She said rumor had it, it's supposed to have the effect of making you lose your inhibitions, circumvent typical walls between viewer and performer, and mesh them into an amalgam of experience that makes this place the influential nightmark that it seems to be. . . . The Tux, brought to the public as a place where fact and fiction are one and the same.

Frankly, it looked like it could just be called a pop cultural acid trip and that would have sufficed. In any case, they made their way to a VIP gully, and it was nice because there were no guards. The site of the gully resembled an encampment on a dirt road trail in pre-industrial America, but the aesthetic integrity was compromised by the seats and the phones. Jean was not complaining. He was complacent about the ratio of cats to dogs.

Rex's red-hived face emerged from the ruckus with a smile best compared to the Cheshire cat in Alice's Wonderland. Must have been a shark; Jean did not know molars were that numerous in the feline mandible. Boy, was Rex glad though and honest to a higher power, so was Jean. Monica was there, too. From her first observation, Jean could tell she was a bit put off by his presence. Settled that with an etiquette peck, sat back, and sipped to get a prime viewing seat for the rabid Harley establishing her bravado, laying down the stakes on her claims of men that thought she was a gold mine. She was. Funny how the roles reversed after a while, with everything, and then could cycle back around. This time, though, it was clear and distinct that Harley was in her natural role, and she had brought Jean as her date, not the other way around. Did not really bother Jean much though. He sure enjoyed her brash tactics and stratagem only a daughter of a general could have in another era. For some reason, perhaps it was the whirlpool of images and sights he had been blended into, mixed up in, and lost without realizing where the exit was, but Jean felt spry, loose, and sprung for whatever may have fallen into his lap at the moment. As long as some work was to be accomplished. Brubaker was conspicuously absent.

The enclosed spaces started to creep more inward than comfort's limits. It had to be the barrage of swarming bloodsuckers and boozehounds that lacked the class to control their liquor intake. And, all in all, Jean's detest of the average mope took little to be let loose in an inebriated state of mind. The two Polish editorial models, Nikita and Vicky, parked themselves on both sides of his legs around the circular couch and proceeded to bust his balls. They were not *that* gone, so it proved refreshing, especially when they got the next two drinks. By this time, Rex had noticed, smiled, and skipped on to the darkness down the other side. As a casual observer, Jean though the route fortuitous. Therefore to the pisser, trailing spectral Rex, shadows nonexistent in the Christmas-lit sphere and at a juncture, the bathroom door and a staircase leading down to black. With a quick look around and duck under the stall doors to ascertain no Rex, Jean proceeded down to the abyss.

Double paneled doors with mirrors one way, Jean's way, tempted curiosity. The locks were open and with a smooth heave, Jean came across a screening room. On the screen a grid of black lines disaggregated the pixels into specified dynamic camera birds' eye views of the club. The grid was five TVs, and the top, bottom, right, and left were mixed while the inner grid space was hitched on sports highlights.

Rex and some anonymous broad were inspecting a computer screen in lap, both of them, as in the chick on his lap, the computer on her lap, and the controls manned by his arms around her. Languid laughs and giggles meshed with the buzz of the bass from The Tux grounds above and behind.

Dodging that encounter, Jean snooped by to the projection room, the control panel in essence, and was baffled at the setup's technical sophistication. Hell, this could have been a professional recording studio. Separate mic set-ups in isolated sound-padded closets, a smorgasbord of knobs, levers, input holes, output cords, and under the oak coffee table was a polar bear rug—its eyes perpetually glaring at the entrance where he stood. Through the doorway and past the rug was another staircase, this one spiraled upward like in an ancient castle, small diagonal steps, but there was no view up or down on account of the beam of metal that directly interrupted that vision.

Jean wiped his brow of accumulated sweat. If his body had had its own speaker box independent of his will, it would have said "Shucks." Therefore, Jean lit a cigarette and made the trek upstairs, a lethargic gait.

Near the top was when he began to hear trailing voices. They led Jean to a chamber like the ones where the damsel is in distress and held in prison until a prince from a far off land comes to save her from any plight. Only this one overlooked the city lights and came equipped with telecommunications.

Harley greeted him, "Jean, come, come, we were just talking business."

Brubaker introduced himself, reserved, remained at the other end of the chamber, and gave a welcoming smile judging the faint adjustment of his jaw line, micro head bow, and eye contact direct. Expected him to be taller, only at 5'11" or so, but the shadows, rather than smother him with their objective presence, looked more like they deferred to his surly demeanor. "Pleased," was all he said. Then, he poured

Jean a drink. He remained querulous, silent, and on second glance, looked as if he had a great weight on his mind, Jean inferred. Brubaker had a lit cigarette in his right hand, and he kept twirling it around and through his fingers the way charlatans do with a coin. It was kind of cool, a kind of cool Jean had not been witness to in some time.

The whiskey was quaint, and Harley gave no misgivings that she would be of assistance. She was a spectator. There was a pause, not a silence, but a pause when he took a drag and flicked the remainder into an oblong ornament that became an ashtray when the flick landed righteous in between two edges.

"I have heard you consult . . ." he initiated. Jean nodded. Brubaker continued, ". . . your references, I consider, trusted individuals to me with high regard," and he nodded to Harley with his eyes.

"Well, don't believe everything they have to say." His head was arched steeply downward and his eyes raised to Jean's level, and to the seated spectator, his mouth extended past his eyes so he resembled a poltergeist, a sad clown specter. But he still had charm.

"I'm not typically morose in first impressions, but my nature now only reflects my present frustration and struggle to cope with the matter at hand, the matter I believe you can assist me in."

So it went.

He opened his mouth a few times, no words, a minute gasp, and another cigarette. He offered Jean one, Jean took it, and he delineated. "I lack the gumption for somewhat shoddy matters, this matter, in particular, concerns my self, my auxiliaries, and yourself, if you accept, the concern being that my lady has gone awry and I cannot be certain she may do harm to not only herself but also to the aforementioned parties. I am afraid it is a grave matter, indeed."

Brubaker focused his faculties on an abstract heirloom. It looked worn by the touch of human hands on the sphere of gold bronze, and he rubbed the orb with tender care and angst. Jean always thought it amusing that more often than not, the prospective client always found a way to heighten the drama and build the suspense before revealing a sliver of insight, or information, or both, that Jean could have bet was the case. Either way, his patience knew how to regulate body language. Jean waited.

Harley fiddled with her mobile. She likely felt Jean's waiting and heard the silence. Without lifting a glance from the glowing screen in hand, "You two share a common bond."—With that, the floodgates were let loose. Brubaker did his best impersonation of Cary Grant's flabbergasted mug, baffled at what sounded like an accusation but was really an obvious elephantine insight into the matter.

He then struck a gaze with Jean. Jean motioned to Harley, "Care to explain?"

Premature clamor about Jean's past with Vittoria only catapulted Brubaker's trust and reinvestment of the situation. Jean could be the white knight, surrogate, via Brubaker's assumption that Jean was emotionally entwined in the outcome of the case. This was no standard job, he had assumed, and with that, trust was to be surely molded to establish what, in essence, was going on.

Now, if Vittoria had skipped off, there were only two places she would remotely consider hiding, escaping to. One was Cairns, Australia, and since it was winter there now, Jean doubted that was the case. The other, the assumption, was not a place but a person, her sister Amelie. Jean put the thought in freeze frame, mind archived.

Brubaker finally settled into an armchair and cooled his jets. With a rickety concoction that involved some powder pills, a splash of pomegranate juice, and a mixer, a hazy membrane enveloped his open-shaded eyes. Harley left the men to get to know each other, she said there was more common ground than either of them could or should assume.

Jean was sick of all these assumptions. Coffee did the trick. Brubaker did his best to inhibit his curiosity about Jean's profession, up to the moment when the concoction distorted his perceptions—Brubaker spewed something like, "It's just that I only imagined this sort of thing in the cinema and have never encountered it up to now in the flesh." Jean tipped his hat at him and passed the comment through one ear and out the other. Despite the narcotics' easing of his mind, Brubaker kept moving about, his knee jumping up and down, his feet tapping, a change of rectal adjustment in the armchair, pacing back and forth, rubbing the bronze orb, almost as if he was obsessive compulsive. Superstitions evolved into taboos engrained, embedded, enfolded, succumbing to the relative blending. His auburn handkerchief had turned dark with sweat wiped off his brow and from what Jean gathered were sweaty palms. At least Brubaker finally realized it, announced he was in order for a good joint followed by a great blowjob. Jean laughed, they smoked, and upon exiting, both proceeded to the playing grounds. One of Rex's models, must have been Vicky, did her duty for Brubaker. Yeah, it had to be Vicky, because it was certainly Nikita that did Jean right.

Harley asked where Jean had been, and Jean ignored her, and there was no more of it. Jean got bored, exchanged information for contacting Brubaker, and left Harley to fend for herself. In the car ride home, Jean realized he had not much work to do regarding his present load. It all seemed to have been presented to him on a platter, displayed for him behind revolving doors on a game show, and was it just a lucky streak or was there something more scintillating as reason that there had been a perfect run of prizes, gems, and diamonds to add to the hoard of information that was accumulating in his case-solving inventory? Then again, it could all be a charade and Jean was the supreme butt of some big joke. But most likely, Jean accorded that his worries were imprisoning his mind in a frenzied paranoia and that it was all hogwash that should be flushed down into an inaccessible sewer. That way, Jean could finish the job and get on with it all.

7

T

TO GET on with it, Vittoria had to be confronted. Jean deemed it confrontation rather than rescue or reason not because of his insatiable hunger for conflict and its merry consequences but really for the previous experience with beautiful beasts at bay. In a corner, they all act with the same reckless abandon. Survival instincts needed to be in tip-top combat order. Not by her own accord, but, in essence, it was all the same that her messenger calls had been contaminating the social and job circles that comprised Jean's recent living and without her quarantined explication of the spiraling facts and rumors, Jean could not be sated, grounded, or relieved.

Jean did his best to remain out of annoyance in the ride over her way. This was all on a limb and now that limb required a background check on the notorious Amelie.

Amelie had lived her life on the mantra that reconstructed the America we inhabit in the postmodern time. It made Jean vomit inside his mouth just comprehending that. Her blood brewed with the innocent idealism of sex, drugs, music, countering any mainstream with the firm belief that by her nomadic tribulations, her self-professed labors of love, and her experimental attitudes in a collective setting were all the realizations of the nouveau righteousness that redefined notions of reality, lifestyle, and fulfillment. Her liberty in life did not result in the happiness pursued by conventional standards. But, here and there, Jean admitted that that made logical sense—she had never masked her pursuits in convention. And she had been proud. However, upon further induction, she had departed from society prematurely, self-exiled on a quiet piece of land to live in peace into perpetuity. This was the last Jean had heard, and this was some years back when Vittoria was still his main squeeze, and they had gone to visit Amelie in her humble den nestled in the coastal beachside community of Carpinteria.

If there was anywhere Vittoria would be staked out, this had to be it. The ride up these ways was blooming with promise, with direction, with gumption. Maybe it was how in the operation of a vehicle, or in a caravan of like-minded individuals, the human body kicked into active mode, streaming the volition to live, to tread through unchartered adventure, and to find some unholy grail to wave at desire at the finish line. The grail was rarely there, but the belief in the sunny side of the Elysian fields through the blight of the unknown always kept Jean going, gave him some hope that the car was Virgil and Jean was Dante emerging out of the static nothingness.

The door was open. There were locks on the doors here. Jean recalled that that was one of the main appeals of the place. Even though the floors had the makings of cold, unforgiving wood, his steps were soft and not foreboding. Amelie was in the same place, too, as last time. It was not déjà vu or eerie to the eye, for this was somewhere to stop and relax. Jean bypassed greeting her and postponed the eventual exchange that he preferred to direct as more a farewell than a hello again. The next room worth a look was through the large opening in the wall. A real estate agent label of the living room would be "suitable," for the room was barren, empty, cold, but not cold in a bad sense. All the windows were covered with curtains jagged with the shadows. Despite this contrast, the shimmer of sun penetrated forth through the skin-tone of the curtains. Whatever dynamism the room was built for was static now. The air was still as a breath held. There was a handgun. Spread on the coffee table were ragged books, ashes, and some tobacco, no butts. Previously entombed, a black and white photo peeked from the bottom corner of the topmost book labeled Cooking with Love. Jean did not reach for the photo but smiled at the cover. The faint scent of cigarette guided him through the room to the south most window and there, the smoke was made visible.

She was on the back adjacent porch. Time was slowed when Jean squeezed in his stomach, gathered his lungs in a breath, and did his best to approach softly and gently. She knew someone, Jean, was there yet did not care or bother to glance up and to the left to see who it might have been. Jean lit a smoke, and their smokes coalesced together in the still air. Jean only observed her through the corner of his eye but could feel some blissful warmth in the moment, at peace. In silence. Jean lost track of the next few moments until she said, "Hey there."—His smile must have been genuine. She continued, "I'm glad it's you."

"I'm glad, too."

Whatever it was that resounded through her, it was always so pretty in the daylight. Womanly photosynthetic vibrancy. Taking a seat next to her on the bench, Jean said, "You must have known I'd hear you'd gone off the grid."—She agreed. With a sigh masked in a little laugh, "You know, I always liked it here, too."

Her response, "It never gets old."

"It never gets you feeling bored."

"Same thing."

She chainlit a cigarette to the dying ember of the original. After her first inhale, she let the cigarette rest in her hand for a while and they stared out at the mirrored crosscut sun in the shallow current lacking waves. She said her mouth was parched, asked Jean to fetch the lemonade if he cared for his own drink and the lemons and the tea were inside, and Jean did. After mention of Monica, the coincidental run-in, a few jabs about nefarious affairs, Jean attempted to hint at knowledge perhaps she could share, but she had the sense to just recap her opinion without framing it in a narrative.

"It's obvious that I'm glad you're here—I already said it. And if the reasons were purely platonic, you would not have come in the first place."—Jean's silence response was enough. She continued, "If you want a warning or a cry for help, or the knowledge that you know I'm worried, take it or leave it. Charlie is not the most controlled of characters and if you get on his bad side, there will surely be consequences. But, he is hard to not want to please." She relayed Jean a story of Brubaker, who she called Charlie, of how a chap of his from earlier times interrupted one of their romantic dinners when touring the Croatian coast. How this guy, let's call him Mitch, tracked Charlie down in despair for he not only feared for his own wellbeing but for the wellbeing of his newly-wed wife. Mitch had been having an affair and had been exposed, or rather, under the threat of exposure, defamation, slander, and subsequent loss of reputation if the photos of him and three high stakes red light district broads had been distributed to the public sphere. His timing in the interruption was most dubious in that they, Charlie and Vittoria, were about to catch the right combination of winds and currents to embark on a tryst in the setting sunscape. Vittoria had not heard it all, but from her natural position in peripheral vision and sound, she gathered Mitch had betrayed Charlie in the past through dishonesty and possibly thievery, when they were younger and quite more foolish and emotionally susceptible to irrational behavior. Be it as it may, Mitch was not a beggar, and Charlie kept up his beseeching gaze. In the snap of a finger, he instructed Mitch to wait on the boat with Vittoria, the boat still at dock, and went to the dockside cafe to engage in some phone calls. Upon his return, after an hour, where what she had just explained to Jean had been better framed, background and all, the sun had already set, the swordfish meal was spoiled, and Mitch's troubles were no more. And Charlie told him not to worry about it, so long as he was aware that a favor was owed. And Mitch was off, the couple's night was postponed, and Charlie never brought up a word of regret, annoyance, or condescension towards Mitch.

Her account of the man known as Brubaker baffled Jean. Was it just an act he had shown up to Jean the night before or did Jean happen to catch him at some sort of rock-bottomed perch? Mind reaction: All he could say was it really disgusted him that he had to cadaverously poach Vittoria's thoughts about her new, more well off, more honorable man—and it sated all his curiosities while making him feel something he could only sum up as shame. Jean kept this all to himself, of course.

She was not wearing any jewelry though. She never really did, but Jean considered it a warm sign that maybe she would take his arm if he played a few more hands right than she. The one tidbit she revealed was that Charlie had been spending a great deal of time at the testing facility in Box Canyon at the Open Door grounds. She told Jean to look on the table with the gun for the photograph, and it showed her magnificently half in and out of a plane doorway reminiscent of a royal lady's grand landing minus the hoarding jackals of lenses and flash lights. The conversation soured Jean's outlook. After such an exchange, Jean knew Vittoria and he could not go back to the wayward bliss of just sitting beside each other. It had to be done, it was okay, he accepted, but he knew he should go. She said Jean could nap, spend the night in the spare room, and she'd make him a hearty breakfast to get an early start upon morning departure, but he made his way out. She asked a favor: for Jean to give Amelie a ride into town for her meditation class. She reiterated that Amelie always took a liking to him and his sentiments. That was that.

Amelie remained silent until they got going in the car. She was faded beyond a normal one. So Jean thought.

Apparently not, because they shared a joint after she made Jean take the long route across the mountain bends before entering town. She had overheard bits and pieces of the conversation with Vittoria and kidded about Jean's diffident guise. Jean let her get her verbal punch in, and it was a relief because he got the impression she had not laughed or gotten her rocks off like that in quite some time. And so Jean asked, "What about the other guy?"

"Him, Charlie. He's a real white knight type. High society sort, too, stiff competition if I ever saw it."

"Remind you of some old flames?"

"Ha, Jean, you could say that. Or you could have said ash." There were ashes spilled on her jeans, and she wiped them clean off.

"I'll tell you one thing though, gal, he's a fine actor."—She was not curious about Jean's meaning. She just said she already knew.

Jean dropped her off on Main Street. It was not for meditation class. Instead, some young rude boy in a lifted truck with a surfboard reeled her in. Still led a double life that one. But she made him stop short, rolled down her window, and gave Jean a gander.

"Just so you know, Vittoria and Charlie are moving to New York at a moment's notice."

"Why didn't she say?"

"I guess she doesn't believe it's actually going to happen until it actually does."

And she was gone.

8

A BOUT THE time Jean was ready to get on the road and back to the urban sprawl, Cheese phoned him, and he answered. Cheese had a use for him up these parts that would collectively benefit an upcoming party that they'd both planned to attend. He had a contact that had defected from his production crew in recent memory now in cahoots with certain American natives engaged in another sort of production and refinement— . . . peyote extracts.

North out of town before Jean hit the next coastal luxury community was a turnoff where the highway suddenly ended and merged into a plain old road. At the second merger, Jean exited and made his way through the mountain pass. Based on his instruction, Jean was to spot certain natural signs to allude the correct direction. These included an array of Xs and Os scattered upon certain road signs. When he passed the road signs that in sequence were XXOX, he'd hit the off road through a hidden causeway. Despite his hesitation, Jean was to bulldoze through a dense forestry of shrubs upon which he'd emerge to a manmade and man maintained road to a reservation. Fate had him accomplish reaching the road with surprising and relieving ease. The shrubbery succumbed to the car's momentum and other than a lingering branch and some leaves in the grill and windshield, his car was unscathed. Just as the sun dipped to the other side of the mountains and the shadow of night smothered the scene, Jean had arrived at his destination. This was Chumash country.

They corrected him, Samala country. It was the one and same thing but language has a way of turning offensive if not applied in a proper fashion or context. This was one of them. They were on the outskirts of civilized territories, and as the darkness seeped all around in the blackening cloudless night, the artificial ray beams extended over the other side of the mountains to provide a canopy against the stars. Jean was bummed. Apparently, this was the Casino, the traditional source of income for the federally approved portion of the reservation. Where Jean was was private, confidential, strictly classified to the few insiders and associates of the clan. Jean was psyched.

The checkpoint at initiation was rather foreboding. They did not seem to have any arms of any sort but when the first guard approached the side of Jean's car window, Jean noticed a bulging hunting knife strapped to a leg holster. He also did not look or seem native as far as Jean's stereotypes could fashion. Jean said what he was instructed to do, "I'm here for the orgy." The hunter complied by opening the gate, and it was as simple as promised. Boy, was this to be phantasmagorical if even a meager fraction of what Jean considered to be in store would come into play.

It was not your random walk in the park. This place came equipped with high tech hydroponic greenhouse setups, but the primary product seemed to be grass and it was confirmed to be grass, after the local guiding Jean around smirked that only a square would think peyote could be cultivated in this climate, at least naturally. To keep his composure, Jean laughed off his remark as if he was an enhanced or just plain informed interested party of the trade. To be honest, Jean was learning as much as ever. The local allowed Jean to sample certain strains that were just cured with the guarantee, "You know there's nothing like medicinal club stuff. This stuff is what we won't even sell to the club. They're not allowed. You're at a level of peak exclusivity and experience."—So he said.

If Jean could imagine what Afghanistan looked like, underground in the caves where Bin Laden allegedly hid and eluded our troops, Jean would fantasize their setup was similar to this one at the secret reservation. They had four different kinds of fruit blenders, all with variations on the superficial design not to mention the cutting blades on the interior and different colored lights and options. One would be surprised how crucial it could be to make sure to use the gray blender, did not observe the brand name nor was it visible, with the dense option to carve out the proper pulp for a fresh grapefruit juice. It had serious ramifications for taste as Jean could only know through first person taste witness testimony. Furthermore, in one of the computer rooms labeled the Hub, the operators were not drones but full-fledged Chumash cyberwarriors with shoulder length hair, tracksuits or overalls, passing around a room length bag filled with vapor as soundscapes of a natural climate, this time the rain forest, played in the background. Jean saw the vaporizer volcano on the center table and understood immediately. What an ideal working environment. So Jean heard, his passcode was specific to the upper echelon of associates, and when a new arrival utilized this passcode, he or she was considered a person to be treated with the utmost care and respect akin to the VIP in the hospitality trade. Lucky for Jean, Cheese was always a connoisseur of these sorts of unexpected worlds.

Before Jean could enjoy himself with reduced responsibilities, he was shown his sleeping quarters, upstairs at the saloon. He called it a saloon because it had all the makings of an old west set, swinging doors in the strike zone of a man at full posture, made of wood like shutters, and a raucous floor arena equipped with slots, digital cards, and real life western accouterments. And up the stairs, in the corner suite, Jean had a bed, a long ways oval mirror, a chest, and a quaint window to look out on the dirt gravel road. There were only two streetlights for three hundred feet.

The faint glow of the casino still carried a solar eclipse subtle light cast on the area, so Jean guessed the streetlights were superfluous. Jean thoroughly enjoyed the timewarp, but the local told him better have a flashlight in case he got lost. With the consideration that he would care to sample the package imported from south of the border, best to take the proper precautions because the local predicted Jean would have an inclination to wander off on his own. Hell, the local trusted Jean to the point where he equipped Jean with a cleaned .38 Ruger revolver. Jean was moved by the guide's trust.

Regardless, it was a bummer to discover that he'd be the lone traveler to the dark recesses of the mind's psyche that night, with no other visitors on the property and the residents cooling off from last week's ritual escapades. Jean's timing was finally compromised, to a lesser degree, but he was in the right head space to engage the hallucinogenic racket on a solo drive.

Now, truth be told, Jean had never engaged in straight peyote, sure mescaline, LSD, 2CI, or your good ole magic mushrooms had seemed to enhance and traumatize his sights forever, but this was a new thing altogether. So he was to expect.

Jean had two options, tea or chew. He chose chew, and it tasted as awful as would be expected. Tolerable though. A slight twinge of nausea subsided after a water refuel, and he got caught up in the joint shared with the local, the guide, Kid. He was god-awfully kind, helped Jean set up a nice campfire out 500 yards or so from the living town area, and stayed through the joint before leaving Jean to his journey with a visceral statement, "When it gets dark, go home."

The back of Jean's throat went home, and he could not tell if it was one minute, ten, or sixty, but the embers played like little angels jumping through fiery encrusted waves, and the dead space between was where the sun-rays got through to illuminate the scene, like the negative in a photograph with every breath consciously taken, the ground beneath and around rumbled softly, and if Jean readjusted his feet against the gravel, the rocks that shifted crashed his audible sensations with a crescendo of low crushing noises.

Eventually, Jean wandered off and chose not to return to the safety of his bed at the distant light for the night-time being. The embers got smaller and smaller and about forty feet out from whence he started, the fire miniscule in depth perspective perceived, vanished, and Jean was alone in the night. The Chumash Casino glow lingered. Coupled with the crescent moon and a cascade of star sights, Jean felt like he was in his own personal observation hall. He thought back to when he was a kid and had been to the Griffith Observatory and how he had believed the place was the center of a universe called cool because whenever he went to the amphitheater that proclaimed the sky was to be filled with stars and light a galaxy, not to discount the planets or the satellites, whenever he looked up in real time in real life and tried to wonder, to dream about the aether, the city lights made them all go away. So there he had it, the manufactured reality looked more appealing, and now that he felt like a newborn head sprung from the spectacle, it was touching to have a wayward reminder that the grand illusion of technology could never surpass the innate carnality of being in a world unscathed by civilization's encroaching binds. Funny though, whenever Jean saw a crescent moon, he could never escape the notion that there was a young boy chillin' in the lunar hammock, fishing for some comet to catch. Working his dreams in the night sky as Jean sometimes did, but, man, could Jean not escape Spielberg's iconography. Fucking brand equity.

It was essentially a classically conditioned pejorative of imagining things for himself that had been usurped, taken out from under, and when Jean saw that crescent moon, he was unconsciously triggered to make the association with the DreamWorks studio. In any case, it made him wonder. by the edge of the tree line, Jean came upon a fruit of some sort, just a tad under the size of a softball, and it felt squishy and the right amount of rough in his hand. Jean tossed it up into the moon when he went out to the flat land and caught it the first three times because he did not throw it too high, he supposed. The fourth time, Jean lost track of the trajectory and it hit him on the head, and he laughed at his clumsiness. The fifth time, Jean went for it and caught it and felt happy. Then, the sixth time, Jean tossed it with all his might upward, and it splattered to his right after what felt like an eternity. The sound sounded unbecoming, like he had intruded upon the natural silence of the night with an utmost lack of care for the peace before him and for more than a couple of minutes, Jean regretted his decision to destroy the atomized fruit that he had labeled a core to his personal monologue. The boom of the gravitational pull made a juicy thud that if had been recorded with a digital rendition of waves, would have reached the upper and lower limits and at this juncture, it felt forced and wrong for some reason. So Jean moved forward and onto a new chapter for his perpetual hallucination to come back to an agreeable steady metronome with the push and pull of his feet with the earth below.

Jean felt like a true traveler, not some mere tourist, but he was probably more the latter even though he preferred to think he was the former. Sure, Jean was by his lonesome, in the natural world, at night, when the predators lurk and his safety was up to his care or lack of, alone, but this remained in the confines of a land where men had long ago established a hegemonic balance of order that if a wild beast came to see him, the sight of his body, Man, the Image, would strike fear in its heart more so than Jean's and its flight instinct would kick in over-drive before Jean could make a decision to fight or flee himself. It was still a nice mindset for the night. At the edge of the tree line nearest to the town area, Jean heard "Hoot, hoot," and a sturdy owl glided over-head, came to a rest at the edge, and remained as Jean passed by. They were on the same page, so he thought.

He got back to the saloon, and it was quiet. Guess it was a weekday, and the few remaining drunks there motioned Jean to help himself. One thing that struck him was that despite his lack of familiarity on a personal level with any of the patrons, they appeared completely nor-mal. By normal, all Jean could think was that there was no hospitality or suspicion or judgment on their part, and if Jean had been sober, he'd probably feel like they were harboring some cautionary instinct that, under the influence, he was too content to be worried about in that mode and setting. A steady shuffling of cards and a few cries of laughter and dice eased the interlude track of the break in the audio-visual trip, and upon depressing his senses with the whiskey, Jean ascended to his bedpost to dream back to reality.

His dreams were somewhat disturbing. Jean was in a train station, and they were all there, the ones involved in his recent life, and a few old faces from when he was a more naive soul, and there was lots of clamor but for what reason remained unknown. And like when a movie cuts or you blink your eyes, a new setting emerged, and Jean began finding himself on some stable ground. Incognizant of any of his other surroundings except for Vittoria's distorted face overlooking his laid out carcass. He thought it a carcass because when he looked downward, his neck buckled and his chin struck his sternum and upon downward sight, Jean saw his left leg gnarled open, tibia visible, like a zombie's. There was no blood running, but the wound looked like it was fresh, and had not been attended to, just allowed to rot. There was no pain other than the visual shock and horror, at his leg and if he moved it, that cagey bone adjusted itself at his discretion.

Jean had no idea what to make of the images when he awoke, but no matter, it felt comforting to have Vittoria there at his side even if it was only a dream. When he got back to the San Fernando Valley, he delivered the goods to Cheesequarters. Cheese happened to be napping so the goods were delivered to some other girl who looked like Monica. Did not bother Jean. He went to Randolph's after a shower, nap, and a splash on the face with some vile aftershave astringent. He felt lost but would never admit that was how he felt to himself. The newswire was eerily stagnant in contrast to the noises that had jittered the media streams the past few weeks since the mystery started. It felt nice, though, a lull and semblance of return to stability, tranquility, order. Rex kept phoning him and leaving voicemails, and the vibrations in his pocket started to bug him so Jean put it on silent. Harley was not around, either. An old schlub approached the bar and asked about her ten minutes later, and Luke the bartender lingered on Yaw when he had said she had taken a holiday to New Yawk. A quick look at the Wall Street paper showcased the developing public offering of Brubaker Airlines under the section Business & Finance. That was why it was all going down there.

Jean checked the Edwards Air Force Base website, and there was a flight tomorrow, midnight, with an open seat for him, so he booked it. Best thing about surviving and not getting caught for dishonorable conduct was these flight perks. Ten bucks, and New York was appointed to the itinerary. Now, that still left the mystery of the junkie and the fate of Hel Lambert, his lot, and the unscrupulous Dohltrey to cut into the fray. Jean kept working out his thoughts. It was not going well so he returned to Cheesequarters. Cheese was awake, and he let Jean borrow a swell SLR camera and a kit, a few papers with production company names like Viewpoint and Clear Pictures, to formulate a material backbone. All in all, this was for insurance, but Jean had predicated his strategy to avoid using any material to reinforce lies that were probably, actually most likely, to be unnecessary and detrimental to the advancement of his knowledge, and hence, the case.

To be honest, Jean was getting annoyed that there had not been any straightforward compelling crime to witness as of yet, and there certainly was no guarantee that one would come to pass soon. All Jean had was scuttling clatters of information that someone could use, benefit, or harm from the distribution of said information. He left a message with Brubaker's secretary about Vittoria's whereabouts and said to send the check to the address given on the invoice he had sent over before the call. He had to have already known the answer, so why the charade of worry, plight, blight, and diffusion of responsibility for a resolution that required no such thing? They had conducted a transaction, though, and that record was permanent as far as Jean could tell. Surely he could spruce up his illustrious resume of past clients, but no matter.

Jean still had an idea.

The traffic was a bummer yet he still made it to the Box Canyon area with ample time for reconnaissance. In hiking attire, cargo shorts, boots, and sunscreened, found a prime viewing window for the front gate to the facility. He did some bird watching in his spare time and stared out at the natural climate succeeding in quieting his fleeting concerns. Lethargy was twice more powerful than prior to the peyote, and he consciously infused his bodily energies through meditative practice accompanied by chaining cigarettes. At around three-thirty,

Jean spotted the Cabriolet the mystery man had exchanged for the Jag departing the premises, and Jean pinpointed the license plate with the use of the Tamron zoom lens courtesy of Cheese. Jean stayed put for a while, meaning he continued his aimless wandering around the shrubbery and Flintstone-like rock formations. He caught a hawk's wings extended in the foreground with the sun in the back setting against the coming shadows of the night over a particular Flintstone rock that resembled a botched globe. A fine sight captured and memorized.

Jean returned the camera equipment to Cheese and felt bad he did not take Cheese up on the offer of a blunt, flick, and sushi with the girls. Jean sought and got rest instead.

His rest was interrupted around ten that night when Dohltrey came knocking at the door. Jean did not ask him how he had found out where he lived because it could not have been too hard for someone like Dohltrey. Dohltrey did not wait for Jean to offer him consensual entry, or a drink, or any gesture of courtesy. In an eye blink, Dohltrey was there, on the couch, causing a fold in Jean's pants that should not have been folded. Dohltrey waited and stared at Jean while Jean fixed a cup of coffee and scratched his back like a sloth.

When Jean noticed this stare, Dohltrey's eyes were bright white, like spotlights in an interrogation room. Dohltrey was not bothering to ash his cigarette burning halfway down and perched in the vicinity between his wiry lips. Still pouring the coffee, Jean asked, without looking back, "What ya got to say? Looks like that makes me guess . . ."

"There's something big on my mind."

With that, Dohltrey unveiled some photographs, black and white, like the old movies, and he defended their credibility in that things were more clear when colors were eliminated. He had to have read Jean's mind. Jean caved. The photographs were standard enough, showcasing Jean with Harley, Rex, and assorted miscreants at The Tux the other night. Brubaker was absent from the collection. Dohltrey hissed curse words when Jean asked, "What's the bother? How's this news?" His mouth snarled with saliva flying in all directions, a few slurps striking Jean's face, and this got on Jean's nerves though he was somewhat amused. Before Jean let him get a start on some logic, Jean said, "Cool your jets. Let's start this exchange over." Dohltrey was not having any of it. He stood up and started pacing and feeling the walls until the one by the television felt friendly enough to touch to lean on. He struck a match to his cigarette and when it got to the cigarette, the match went on. He cursed to himself. Took his hat off, threw it to the couch, and started the process again. Here it went:

"What I am about to tell you will put me in a most serious bind. Contract violations, lawsuits if this gets out, that is, unless they get to me first."

"Dynamo."

"Bingo."

"Let her rip."

"As you probably have put the pieces together, Brubaker is a legacy client . . . his father was an immediate investor when the company started up and junior has become a client we, off the record, label a liability. Now, that's not necessarily a bad thing. Liabilities create more opportunities for our services to develop into unforeseen circumstances and allow for greater reward due to the coupling with the greater risk."

"Skip to the important stuff. These photographs don't say anything."

"Simmer down, sleuth. This is a web of interlacing networks that you certainly cannot begin to contemplate."

Lit a cigarette in response.

"It all began seven years ago when Brubaker left Melkore, the commodities giant, to begin his entrepreneurial game. He backed a few petroleum suppliers, refiners, and metals manufacturers and handlers, and upon stringent disciplinary leveraging of the global capital markets, his independent business expanded its reach—primarily through acquisitions before the final merger into Brubaker's Holdings today, hence, the imminent launch of the airline. You see, the IPO debuting on the NYSE is rather unprecedented in that the company, despite a presence in the public arena for the seven-year period, has conducted its business outside of American borders. This has created a momentous ascent to equity value and subsequent high market capitalization and rather liberal asking price at forty dollars per share. Of course, this pricing scheme puts Brubaker's investment in stock equity as a stake of four billion dollars. Now, despite such a stake and the necessary political underpinnings to back such support in the American markets, Brubaker has been most notorious in his petty crimes. I'm not referring to the domestic abuse accusations, though that is a certain sin. Or the Norco's habit, or the reckless endangerment accounted for by his personal acquaintances, whether it be in the air, boat, or any type of motorized vehicle. You see, the risk is that this guy talks. Government representatives have been closely eyeing his activities on a day-to-day basis, surveillance, wiretapping, tails virtually constant, for he has been under suspicion of the violation of antitrust laws on the federal level. Hell, he could have treason under his belt for all Dynamo knows. But you may just consider this hearsay, and I cannot do much more to convince you otherwise. . . . Let's just be clear, these photographs are sourced from the government—my guy at the NSA whose been feeding me the progress and status updates regarding the government's snooping, which luckily, is always a step or three behind Dynamo's and subsequently Brubaker's—hence, you've been caught in the crossfire. You're marked and the consequences of unwarranted, documented attention can prove most dubious. I need not defend that sentiment."

Jean could not agree more with this sentiment, but then again, this guy was not helping his own cause to be trusted. This smelled of bullshit like city sewers clogged up by too much of it. But Jean let the paraphrased consumer report float about and mesh with his mind's logic. Paranoid notions, perhaps of delusion but maybe of some real legs riddled the information absorption with asterisks and underscores.

Jean studied Dohltrey's move, his face most clearly, and it was blank with curiosity, no faint shimmer of perspiration on a brow. Neither a deep gulp indicated by a neck movement nor a scratch nor a fixing of the hair. He was staunch. Jean remained unsure.

"What do you expect of me? I'm already caught in the mix somewhere in the middle, and I intend on seeing this through to completion. There is no way else I can accept my role and responsibility."

"You sure can whip up the proper notion of chivalry when the time calls. I see it now."

"Don't ever expect anything less. You have to ignore the quibbles of apathy flooded by the steady liquor streams in the night."

"If you took my statement like a faint jab of sarcasm, don't. You are aware of who I represent, and so on their behalf, we've prepared a healthy resolution to the predicament, clogging up business with unnecessary complications and possible detriments to Dynamo's interests."

Jean could see where this was going, but he did a keen self-check to look surprised. Dohltrey reverberated, "We are prepared to offer you a considerable payment for your time and services rendered contingent upon your resolute resignation from the cases involving Mr. Charles Brubaker, Junior, and concurrently, Miss Vitti." With that, he placed a manila colored folder on top of the photographs and the envelope slit opening revealed it full of Benjamin Franklins. Dohltrey continued,

"This is our initial sign of good faith. Think it over and let us know by the end of tomorrow."—He started to go.

Jean almost said, "You've got to be kidding," but he restrained himself. This sort of changed everything. Jean had had his reservations about Dohltrey's agenda, but that was a genuine pitch if he had ever witnessed one, let alone, been the recipient of one. However, an easy buck to forget his problems and his clients' problems was not enough to scare him silent. There was more to be done, and Jean figured there'd be more snoops watching him and recording his moves so as to not interfere with theirs. Jean left the money and photographs on the table for a while, but before he went to bed, he shredded them with his hands, the way a semi-safe citizen shreds his receipts after folding them to prevent any threat of identity theft. And right before he went to bed, Jean shot a message to Harley, "East?" and she replied, "Meet ya there."

In spite of their professional experience, Dynamo was to be a nagging parasite going forward. The Dynamo itch was passively alleviated at Jean's discretion the following morning. Dohltrey informed Jean to check his bank statement in an hour and his compensation would be agreeable then. By then, the cab out to Edwards had picked Jean up from the beachfront lot, and Los Angeles County was behind in the mirrors.

As if Jean was the lucky winner of a lottery, Dohltrey bashfully pried over the phone, "Now what are you going to do?"

—Jean remarked, "Take a vacation."—Some vacation.

There were lots of tired faces and a few higher ranking ones on the flight east. Time sucked distance into its vacuum, or perhaps it was the other way around. When Jean came to, the water out the window looked Atlantic, darker, more choppy, and he still was not certain how he'd make out.

It was nice not having to go through the typical channels of cattle herding through the public gates and baggage claims and subsequent cabs queued up, and in an insignificant amount of time, Jean was at the Warwick across the street from the Museum of Modern Art for check-in. He paid cash, the cash Dohltrey had balked for his taking. Before Jean called it a night, he took a mean shit on the second floor lavatory adjacent to the lobby and on the way up and down the stairs, he greeted the motionless faces of yesterday's stars and starlets. The photo framed of Rita Hayworth always got him, way more than any Mona Lisa could. Biting narrow eyes that screamed seduction and allure. But shucks, he still could not describe it adequately. If you ever find yourself thereabouts, see for yourself, and Jean would recommend visiting the loo before taking notice. After the walk by Rita down to the lobby, Jean had the bellhop take his bags up to the room, tipped him handsomely before he went up, and made way to the lounge. It had to be the same bartender as the last time he had been here, unless they all went to the same barber and had the same languid sagacity in their voices. His name was Al, and he started Jean out on some Glen Livet. It was chill that no patrons were markedly loud, but it was a shame no one could use the place for some smokes and wonderings. So Jean stepped out to 54th Street for a smoke and avoided the alienation of a grand American boulevard with wide sidewalks and no walkers that was the Avenue of the Americas. Even though it was getting late by now, the stick of the summer still poached his pits and pelvic region with musty perspiration. Yep, the New Atlantic summers. Global warming, you see, had radically shifted the climate in these parts, most particular, as now, summers in the city waywardly vacillated between major highs and lows, some minor ones, too.

Jean could only assume the oscillations had gotten more pivotal and biting, as things, in their entirety, tend to move at faster rates and relative outcomes come to light ahead of time in this environment unlike any other place he had experienced up to this time. There's a reason they call them city miles—it's the way time just goes away into oblivion, not the uncanny accumulation of superficial aging features. But Jean guessed that happens to a lot of folks out here, and they are all in your face every day so you get to see it, not imagine it. All in all, Jean felt great being back.

Something Jean could never wrap his tongue around was the taste of tobacco in the humidity, it was more delicious east than west. Western smoking was dry, parched, and lacked certain subtle flavors that the tongue could pick up on in the humidity. He just got used to it. Got him every time. About halfway through the cigarette, a trying to look sophisticated type of brand, five inches taller in heels that didn't seem to impede her confident strut, flowing robes of black satin and leather and an orbital focus on her neckline tied together by an ethereal gem worth more than a Mercedes. Yeah, Jean's balls were sticky in summer, but he still got to eye some mimetic form of a magazine girl in the flesh walking by, leaving a trail of potent stillness only interrupted by the disappearing smoke in her hand. There she went again, this time though, it was a different type, going the other direction, not too tall, more voluptuous, as in a proper Coke bottle, her hair flowing and brown the way he preferred, a few curls in it towards the ends by her breasts and when she passed by her opening in the spaghetti strap coalescing skin with lingerie and everlasting hair. Illusory reference: Alice in the 2004 film *Closer*, and the picture is clear. If not, look it up, it's worth the time.

There were so many Gorgons here, and it sort of scared him. Not in an intimidating way but in the way that made him fear taking too many cookies out of the jar and so he avoided buying a jar or filling it up with cookies for fear of overconsumption. It was one of those feelings that persisted, the push and pull, the visual sensation of there always being more and more and more and no end in sight, unless the bank account went into the red, or there was some blackout and society crashed and ground to a halt.

Jean admitted to himself that he missed this place and his energy was on overdrive just by people watching the streets in silence. Striking eyes with one of those two was enough. He could control himself and a cold shower was next in line to get ready for the next day at a sprint. He still preferred to catch eyes with the other.

9

THE MORNING paper read: "Prepare for Lift Off," Brubaker Air was coming in hot, triple A rated by the underwriters, and chunky stakes bought by now preferred stockholders such as the banks that own this country and the world. The summer weather was sticky scorching and before all the brokers went on vacation, this was to be the last Moby Dick to unleash to the hordes of traders, hunters, and dreamers of numerical scores.

I stayed in all day, got three orders of room service, and arranged for a car to be waiting outside the hotel, activated by a code I could enter on the driver's side door. The code was 6-9, 6-9, 1. The ticker on the finance channel careened by, left and left and left, and the Bru stock, symbol BRUK, broke out at a reasonable 46.00 dollars a share, and other than a hiccup dip for fifteen minutes before lunch hour, ballooned upward to close at 52.75. About 4:45 P.M., after the markets had halted, was when Harley bombarded my phone. I refer to the hotel phone, in that she had shown up in the lobby upset by her isolation in riding a digital rush so high that by the time it was market close, her girlfriends had retired to get a siesta and a reboot for the night of festivities, while Harley, locked in Go-mode from travel, spoil, and cocaine, saw no end in sight.

But, hey, she could count on me, I admitted. I met her at the sculpture garden across the way and there were fresh drinks awaiting our consumption. There were also two empty ones by her half full one. It was kind of cozy in the corner where we sat but the legions of sight-seers and observers took away from the aesthetic of the mimetic forms of antiquity coupled with the smooth tile grounding and dark hued waters geometrically arranged around the tile. But the shade was key, and so the sweat did not get to me.

"There's a party tonight."

"Only one?"

"And a dinner before, and then God, no, not only one, there's an after party and if we make it to daybreak, we can take the helicopter for a spin. You see, this is the exclusive tip, courtesy of Charlie, because the rest of them drunkards will only be onlookers on the nautical vessel below. There will be jet skis though, and if you never jetted around the Hudson, trust me, you would know not to match the experience otherwise. But, oh, oh, good great Mother Mary, how my fortune has catapulted to gracious Godly heights. Am I some reincarnate Athena or what, Jeanny, Jeanny— JEANNY."

I took a deep breath around where she started talking about the helicopter and the jet skis and let my attention span to the trees breezing in the skyscraper wind.

"Hey, sleuth, how you feel about taking me downtown?" She knew how to get my attention. Sleuth kinda bothered me, when the tone struck the wrong chord. It was okay, my haphazard wander, but I responded, "Not in a lifetime," and she rebuked, "You must've slipped your mind with that remark."

"Don't remind me , sister."

The sister mark got under her skin, and she shifted her seat and told me she needed to powder her nose. Real inconspicuous. She didn't go to the bathroom, though, she unhinged her lipstick mirror ornament and with a tic and tac, and snort, it was all done in a jiffy. What a gal.

Apparently, no one really noticed. She interrogated me. "So what are you here for?"

"Keeping an eye on ya."

"Bullshit if I ever been to Mijas. Tell me your play."

"If I did, I'd have to disappear, no actually, I'd have to make you disappear."

"Or I could just vanish? You'd like that, hunk, huh?"

"As long as you remember that silence is golden."

"Hm, don't kid yourself, buster."

"I never kid about my work."

"Oh, my, the buster doesn't kid about his work . . . the work just makes him kid himself. Oh la la."

Ten minutes later, we were heading downtown. Right about that last pony snippet she shot at me in the garden, I was thinking while driving that it would have been so fitting for a bird to fly into her head right then and there. But, hey, she did manage to appease my grumbling testosterone with an appeal to the future that would be the night, her girlfriends. But, like I said, work was nothing to kid about, not yet. She goofed on me for having a nuisance of a car when we could just hail livery cars or hire a personal driver for the time being, but I told her I preferred to have my own means of escape at the time when it might come. She shook her head but continued inhaling powder into the ever growing crater that was her left nostril. I told her she should switch off, and she told me not to meddle in her ritual. When we got to the FDR, I had my day in the setting sun. Kicked the gear up and high-tailed it down and she spilled some on her blouse and then licked it off before she butted her head against the headrest. That was my doing, ha ha.

When we got to 14th Street the traffic killed the rush. There were quite a lot of snapshot worthy scenes through the car windows, like the family barbecue at the East River Park, the baseball game at one of the park's fields, and a plane in the background between two tenement buildings and a tree branch in the foreground bottom to frame it cinematically.

But the traffic was a killer. We stayed put in the Alphabet City because the area west had been pile driven to shopping mall status and so even if Loisaida Avenue was only a starving beast soon to go extinct in neighborhood character and charm, it would do for now. I wasn't paying attention too much, but the knowledge of my idealism in the act of driving an honorable route made me brim with pride. I dropped off Harley at this speakeasy above this basement shithole called Home Sweet Home off Chrystie Street and due to her description of the place as a low key swanky retreat for Wall Street players situated behind a posh art gallery, I declined the invitation. She said she expected it and even if, there would be somebody that could improve my prospects, and it didn't matter much. That time would be to come when the sun was fully down and the street-walkers switched out for the nighttime replacements of smut disguised as glamour.

There was a lot of traffic so I ditched my car below Delancey at the lot off Broome between Norfolk and Clinton. Call me a mainstream guy, but I felt suave pulling in with the DB4 Aston Martin made publicly cool thanks to Sean Connery as James Bond. The guy named Bob, at least that's the American name he went by, eyed me up and down to see if he could gain an understanding of the context that such a ride would pull up to these isolated parts. South of Delancey, and especially east of Essex, the Lower East Side still had the makings of a local neighborhood and through gentrification was seeing to its eradication, there were still spiritual guardians that were formed by the workers of the neighborhood to reinforce the locals—only attitude. I told him I was keeping track of the mileage by the tally I made with my finger on the dash and tipped him righteously so he'd look after it for a while, and with gumption at that.

I asked him for a light, and he relented and then asked because curiosity can only be held back for so long when he asked about the ride and my doings. I responded, "I'm an operative for the gaming industry."—His eyes bolted alive. "You, see, I've been following a totally rude fugitive player out of the Boardwalk and as you can see, I gotta find him in this dumpster of a maze."

He told me to check out the Triad game behind Tropical Bar for some talk about whereabouts about those types of games here, they were still illegal in the city limits, but was glad to be of assistance to me in any which way he could or thought he could. I thanked him and made my way South, farther downtown.

I had gotten so used to lying I framed it now as colluding. See, with collusion, two or more parties could create a conspiracy, secret, never explicitly spoken in stark nature, but the purpose was common and forthcoming for the parties participant. So, thereby, if I lied or deceived in any which way to extract information or gain an upper hand or just ensure some sort of beneficial outcome to mine truly, I was thereby in collusion with whoever I was swindling at the time, whether they knew it or not, and they certainly did not. But either way, I did my best to remain civil and courteous, at least on the surface. Respect was a superficial behavior, and people weren't so bad. Just keeping on because what else could they do? What else could I do? Well, I tell you I could get a beer.

All in all, when people get drunk together, especially when they're not close, the truth gets stretched to serious elastic qualities and by the end of it, who knows what might be set in stone or just floating on murky waters before melting into falsehood and oblivion. But, I'll get to the drunk. First off, I knew I was not meeting my self-compliant quota of labor and progress so I fast forward to the night. Lurching up the sedentary streets of Chinatown after dark, the garbage skipped about the curbsides and acid rain puddles. When I had been seeing to my soberness with shot-beer combination antidotes, a passing shower of serious magnitude had riddled the area with gusto and as a result, the trash seemed to be playing with itself along the sidelines.

I forgot the name of the place, but it was on Ludlow Street near Grand so still below Delancey but clearly before reaching the aborted child of 57th Street and the Chelsea galleries situated on the Ludlow block between Grand and Broome and Delancey, respectively. It was on the West side of Ludlow and maybe it was called Mercutio's, but I went up the stairs and behind the front eating tables to the back with the wide expanse of wooden dance floor and up the stairs to couches to sit, brood, and devise a strategy for what the hell I was doing there in the first place. One thing about these places buried under sky rises or more humbly put seven-floor walkups was that if you find yourself in a place of business with disposable cash and you're willing to spend, no one bothers you or tries to determine the purpose of your visit. This was one of those times and places. The suit didn't hurt my chances.

But the scenery did not strike me, people wise or any other wise, so I caved to meet Harley at the Wall Street backdoor parlor, and it was what I expected, which was a good thing.

Harley was not doing me any favors so I ambled around the premises before deciding the crowded back room was lacking comfort. Thereafter ordering a whiskey way too pricey, I found myself in the full front gallery space. It was equipped with the standard hardwood floors, white walls, evenly spaced works of some stature, and bright 5500K lights too bright to stand under or to get close to the works without breaking a sweat. About fifteen minutes passed, and I was stuck in a corner mesmerized by this array of Christmas tree ornaments arranged in such a manner as to comprise a reindeer. Perhaps the circular ornaments had been various colors prior to their arrangement and final presentation, but now they were a solid silver metallic shade, and in the multifaceted reflections my spectral viewing plane made the exhibit look infinite. To be specific, the decadent heathens had begun to migrate to the front room to get a good old drunken showing and inspection of the aesthetic wall accessories.

Not to be disrespectful to the artists, but this was how these vagabonds were checking them out one by one, in little cliques of three to six, never for more than ten seconds before continuing their inspection of every possible selection. If any artist was there in the flesh, he or she must have been feeling something worse than moroseness, hence dread. I could feel for the posturing artist, but nonetheless, dread is a feeling one learns to cope with and identify as something to bypass as fast as possible, no matter how much harder that may seem to accomplish.

Back to the reindeer. Something about the disco ball effect the ball deer was giving me was hypnotic, all these swirling lights within the curvatures of the metallic orbs; for instance, yuppie hipster trio on the left moving forward and then right and in the next orb over, the same thing but with a ketamine tilt of the whole scene, and once I got over a few more orbs, I was all in reverse. This reminded me of the time I first got really baked in front of a lava lamp in a dark room, and I was by myself. Regressive flashbacks to times of less wisdom severely embarrass my ego in the face of my id, and luckily, just as the embarrassment became clear and distinct status obvious was when Harley emerged onto the picture plane, and we got on with the night's check-list. So we left. I am still considering cutting this out because of the shameful cousin of dread leading me to spontaneously combust some brooding thoughts of handicapped mental faculties. But, so, we left.

On the street by the park, Harley was arguing with a couple of girl-friends whether or not to go fetch the Aston from the lot and pull up to the next venue in style, or like upstanding citizens of the rank, get a limo off the street or acquire an Escalade through mobile communicative means. I took the opportunity to finally glance at my phone that I had intentionally put on silent mode, alerts off, to close off my person from electronic public access. This had been the right call, the silent mode, upon re-engaging with my phone at that time. The front screen lit up with various alerts through various mobile streams, like messages (text), messages (voice), and calls (missed).

That was one thing about a West Coast base, the time difference. If considered an eastern folk member, any call received would automatically be three hours later received than the westerly folk base, and thus, could be ignored or missed until the following day, into perpetuity. But, be it a West coaster, those that side of the land had extra breathing room awake and alert to hound me for their wants and needs. Those in question were Lambert and his hellacious references, Yung Cheeseburger and Rollins, James Rollins. Luckily, Cheese was busy so he only left a slick message to get in touch when available and that was that. But, besides the off-chance notification from Rex about logistics for the upcoming production and from that Polish broad he had introduced me to in addition to Monica urging me to vouch for her participation, Helmut pounded away at the keys and invaded my cool little screen with concern.

I checked my voicemail first because I had a particularly irritated reaction to the obnoxious icon that made itself constantly known and visible, present on the screen until the messages were dealt with. Hel sounded in over his head, asking what he was to do, if he should accept the offer, if he should renege, if he should skip town, if he should just fire me and get on with his paranoia. I felt partially responsible, I admit. But, nevertheless, I ignored what he had to say in its entirety, and if you don't believe me, check my phone records. Upon final deletion, the phone vibrated with potent urgency, and Hel's number popped on the screen. Clicked Ignore. Settled that.

Now, for the text messages, from an unknown undisclosed number, claimed he the sender was James Rollins, and from the 510 area code, I assumed it to be forthright, and he said, "Mane, do me a solid and call up Lambert, cause he keeps bugging me."—That was enough to change my intent. Up on the next half block those boozehounds were still cavorting and skipping around in heels causing an atonal ruckus on the Chinatown / Soho border so I guess now was the worst time to do the best thing. Call Hel up.

Rollins and I had met in Cabo doing a stint of hospitality for a beachy sea resort. He skipped out prior to this hurricane that was disastrous in effect and from then on, we vanished from any physical presence in each other's lives. Regardless, I owed him more than just a favor. Least I could do was damage his reputation indirectly by being a putz and ignoring a client he had referred to me. In this case, Hel picked up after the first ring, as I tried him at his place of business even though by this time, it was after hours. Must have been an instinctual hunch. I tended to have those now and again and some other times, too. Despite my social inebriation mixed in with so much stimuli to process, and filter out in my current surround scape, Hel's shrieky voice cancelled them all out. I stopped walking and lost sight of the pack of partygoers. On the other side of the Bowery, still on Broome Street, the pack turned a corner left, and so south down Elizabeth Street, and I told Hel to cool his jets, he had that problem by golly every time I phoned him, so I could order an Old Roman cocktail from this place, coincidentally called the Randolph on Broome, and I could sip the rye mixture on the porch area while he spilled his beans to my unforgiving silence . . . So it had come to pass, another offer, another threat, and a reappearance of the dapper junkie. This time, he was out for blood, and demanded his '84 Jag back, minus any processing fees. He was apparently outside as Hel recited his dilemma, and this was happening in real time. Whatever in the hell Hel was getting at, I told him with blunt force to bite his tongue and listen to my instructions.

He did as I asked, so I believe, because after he allegedly put me on hold, for ten minutes or so, he had come back to the speaker box. What I had ordered him to do was simple. The customer was always right. Who knows what, at least being in Lambert's shoes, so act accordingly. He did. He gave him an advance on his refund, collateral as such, so as he could inspect the Cabriolet for reacquisition but before providing the Jag, it'd require maintenance because he sold the claim that he had taken the car for personal use. Nonetheless, his number one prerogative was to please the customer, this time, revealing his true identity, so he said, albeit, probably a fake name, Sean Moser, so upon exchange of the paper documents curtailed with signatures of identification, the Jag would be delivered promptly to Moser's requested location and that would be delivery at his best and most convenient time. Moser apparently took the news with ease, and Hel was dumbfounded by his acceptance of this strange turn of claims, but shit had been put into motion. Moser was off the premises, and Hel was still breathing, panting on the other side of the invisible wire.

I almost had it figured right. Instead of delivery requested to a personal residence, the location was the Open Doors testing facility out in Box Canyon. But the one request that gave me a hint of a chill was that demand, verbatim from Hel, that he be the one to personally deliver the Jag. We needed time, and I told Hel to freeze over at his place of safety and shelter for the time being, take care of the Jag maintenance in the meantime, and prepare and expect my return within the next week. He said he would have to close shop, and I told him, if he did close shop, this would be a promising development for the airline corporate people who we already assumed were watching his every move. But, hey, if he began to relent, they would ease up and allow him to come to a proper decision to benefit them.

The assumptions were right on track . . . but onto the present environment. I told Hel I had to go, my Old Roman was finished and Harley had been flashing my phone for the past five minutes when I had been with Hel so we cut the connection.

I had an itch in my crotch area so I went to the bathroom inside when I picked up. Midstream after adjusting the undergarments to be itch free, Harley finally got her voice in on the mix. Simply put, I had gotten left behind, and my name would be at the second door for the party, but I'd need strict directions to get to the first door, and entry would only be allowed if I gave the password, "Bulworth."

This lent some intrigue to the endeavor, but I thought it best to take my time, as I had an urgent desire for dollar dumplings and a fruit drink concoction that could buy me ten orders of said dumplings. Made the necessary stops off Eldridge for the dumplings and off Rivington for the juice. The time was about eleven and a fight broke out between some Ivy type derivative punks, V-neck sweaters, seersuckers, and Sperrys. It was entertainment, at its finest. Reckless American abandon. When the juice was finished, I made my way south and fetched the car.

Work mode. If you believe me.

10

T HE DIRECTIONS guided me upward and westward via the West Side Highway. The initial entry was delayed by the guard gate at the parking facility at Pier 17 Chelsea Piers. This capitalist mausoleum had always been akin to a commercial development more common in a suburban climate contingent upon wide expanses of space, never-ending parking lots, and a healthy influx of consumers. Simply put, it was a destination on the island of Manhattan that enabled one to get the illusion of escape from the city hypnosis and trance because one, it was on the edge, two, they had huge parking lots, and three, it was un-characteristically quiet amid the great beams of metal and glass that smothered the peripheral senses.

I parked at the lot by the Sky Rink and there were a couple boats at dock, yachts specifically, and two of them had lights on them with signs of farther life forms cascading through the windows behind the cur-tains. I knew I had to discover a certain staircase, but the entry point eluded me at first attempt. I appreciated the suburban illusion when I bumbled down the causeway south, past the docks and with ceilings so high, and the people count at zero, I could enjoy a cigarette in a relatively indoor public space. It was fresh. Three quarters of the way down the causeway, I caught myself staring at the golfing store when I heard a ruckus in earshot on the other side of another parking lot. That was when I caught sight of narrow, muscle strung legs, stressed on stilettos and sinewed with flesh against leather and nylon, that I knew I was on the right track. They walked hand in hand, a legion of sluts.

They were down ahead on the next causeway, snarking relief at their mobile phones when they reached a door and an imposing black man relieved them of their disorientated wandering. I couldn't hear if they used a password or not, but who cared when they looked that way at that time? I followed the trail.

When I reached the door, it was closed, unmarked. Some tooting from cars, looked like limos or towncars, came from the parking lot at the other end of this other causeway that I now found myself within. When did these lots end? Guess I really was in suburbia. —There was no knob on the door, but I noticed a keypad equipped with numerical buttons and a voicebox. I buzzed. A camera above my head rotated to life and inspection, the little red circles forming a circle around the moving black lens. It zoomed on me like a pupil dilated in hallucinatory ecstasy. I conceded, "Bulworth," and greeted the click! unlocked door with pleasure.

The stairs inside the temple of modernity opened to a back entry point of a long wide hallway, concrete floors. A steady dirge of bass echoed and pronounced louder the closer I got to where I was going. I got a rush of vertigo. I was just awakened to find myself in a great industrial complex like a convention center or the London Millennium Dome. My feet kind of ached from all this walking, but I ignored it after an instant and let the dirge guide me onward. A skimpy young thing done up head to toe came out of a wall and looked either way, did not notice me, and started the squat of urination. Punchy lot this crew must be. She turned the other way when I got to the opening through the wall, and I thought how great it would be to just nudge her forward and let gravity do the rest. Hey, she was cute. Especially from behind.

The opening was just that, floor to ceiling, and no sign of doors in a conventional sense. More a temple opening that remains open for permanence in scope and all that comes along with the signs of power for architectural opulence and design. Lights refracted off of umbrellas hitched up on poles stabilized by handbags and they flashed, mostly for five-second bursts, but there was just enough flashing on and off in different sections to destabilize my senses. Especially with the bass. This had to be a green screen room, a room where anything could be made visibly possible in a live unity with digital rehashing and the lively forms on the set reinforced this notion. Some street-walker types of kids had skateboards and were yodeling about with tricks banging and clashing metal against the surface. Chicks cavorted smoking and drinking to coax their bodies in sensuous motion. And great guffaws of lackadaisical bliss meshed with the electronic dirge turned chant, metamorphosing into a flurry of overstuffed gluttony. Some life form shot me into awareness with the flash and click of his perverse cannon of a camera, and I meandered about until I could find a counter where there would be liquor. The bartender or the guy behind the counter was getting sucked off, so I poured myself a heavy glass of scotch. I put an energy drink in my pocket for safekeeping. I did not see any couches in the foreground, so I made my way to the back, and when I got there, it became the foreground and a couch presented itself to me thanks to the leathery glint in the shadows. Where was Harley? My phone did not inform me. Some bloody eyed rascally fellows were deconstructing the glass table by the couches via snorting techniques. It was only a sight for cocaine and the arrangement was one of true delicacy. The powder had a zigzag assortment of mounds, Olympian in relative size and presence, the zigzags looking like rivers on a map of white translucent terrain.

Accepting of my invitation, I came in strong with an avalanche of the K2 relative mound and left Everest to my host. His name was Bobby, and he had the shakes bad, not that he noticed or cared to. This was high-grade product, and when I was in the zone, they giggled, took fingers to nostrils simultaneously, and I wasn't sure if it was just a habit of the moment, but I did the same and wiped off a powdery excess. Some white reindeer all right. The red bull popped out now and intake commenced at a healthy momentum. Locking eyes could become an art, especially under this particular influence. So it came in the form of something you imagine, or rather, recall through recesses of easily accessible memory, probably from a print advertisement or a commercial, but there she was in the flesh because New York made this some dream to be expected in reality.

I made my way and in five minutes we were necking at a voracious pace. Hell, I was not even thinking, just functioning, being part of the crowd. I don't regret it by any means.

Vapidity could be charming. Her name was Bree or Lee. She had cute cross eyes, alien type of foreign hot, and noteworthy dimples. The rest you can imagine for yourself, but her image hit the mark on all fronts for general approval. The flying colors beleaguered my senses, and I continuously increased my focus on her rump. Thank God she had some hips because if I felt cagey bones in the pelvic region, my goods would have taken a turn for flaccidity. I got a tap on my shoulder, and it didn't go away, it kept persisting. It was Harley. She looked like a schoolteacher then and there, only in the eyes where I was forced to make connection. Whatever, she made herself a scene and walked away. Like I was hers or something, the bravado on tha' broad. I continued my descent into Bree-Lee's bosom, and we didn't have to talk, we were animals and our territories converged all over one another.

I kept the foray relatively short, gave her my number, told her where I was staying, and left the door open for an early morning rendezvous. The party was by no means dissipating in splendor or pumped enthusiasm; rather, the throngs of attendees were getting more rowdy, glasses breaking via heel stomps, seminal tosses, and collisions of thrusting and refractory motions. But the lights were really fuzzing my vision. Went to some makeshift bathroom area outside the door, past the squatting girl's remnants now in a disintegrating piss puddle, and wiped my brow after a face wash. Out of the stall emerged Harley and some harlequin accessories. I do not know why they proceeded to the bathroom for their fix based on my public display and the displays of innocent drug love in the party arena. Hey, I guess she still valued some semblance of privacy. She and I struck eyes through the mirror. She wasn't a schoolteacher now, just a competitive dame with a predilection for drama. Made my mouth salivate; despite energy drinks giving the consuming user cotton mouth, I experienced a proverbial bodily reaction, and my libido wanted what it wanted, regardless of that other Bree-Lee option that was attractive enough. Harley hissed, hard to get. I ignored them superficially, but took the body language for what it was. In the hallway to reenter the splendor, Charlie himself and I struck shoulders on a chance, then hands on a surety. He was sky high, but it didn't seem like drugs. We were shifting venues momentarily and it'd be best if I came along with them. Accounting for the car and what not, he looked around to heighten the suspense and maybe to make sure no one was looking, but he proposed we skip out unseen and take the ride for a glory run.

What could I say?

*   *   *

—Uptown on 10th Avenue. "Be careful how you go."—Sarcastic sounding.

"Am I being careful?"—I wasn't. Red lights flurried across all lanes, and I beamed the car ahead with taut maneuvering ability.

"Don't you hate that?"

"What do you mean?"

"When you can't see ahead?"

"Depends on what's ahead."

"But you still would prefer an open range in view."

"That's one way to put it."

"I always feel like it's a conveyor belt, the road in the city, but the lights do something about that."

"They make you forget you're stuck."

"I guess I'm blinded by the city lights."

"Well, at least you can see what's around."

"But what's ahead?"

"Your memory, intuition. Whatever."

"Care for a smoke?"

"Yes, if you mind."—Charlie lit up two, handed me the first. I went east towards the Park. Here, when we got there, there were fewer lights.

"Didn't see your lost and found one where we just were."

"Ha, keeping an eye out, for me I assume . . ."

"Naturally. It's not a conflict of interest. It's kinda the opposite."

"I'm glad you were able to get out here. I haven't even considered how or why."

"Even straw dogs need vacations."

"Naturally."

Silence, smoke.

"You're the talk of the town."

"Now I just gotta be tomorrow's hero."

"So that's what you're going for, eh?"

"I have a lot of chips on the table."

"Isn't that why you just took them off, going public?"

"It's merely liquidity matters. But that's not the issue."

"You feel good about it?"

"That should have been rhetorical, even though it sounded like it was not. Of course, but sure, I don't feel any bit different than beforehand, minus the stresses of protocol."

"I'll just imagine."

"You caught me at a most vulnerable time when I hired you. Now, that things have swung in my direction, and with the assistance of this ride, I'm hoping you won't put me for a romantic fool."

"Quite the contrary. Don't kid yourself. I didn't see any tears and fears out of hand at The Tux."

"You're just being civil."

"Whatever you want to call it."

"Let's make down Fifth in all this vain glory."

" 'Bout time I asked you where this was going."

"Just go down Fifth."

"Light me another one of those before all these lights turn green."

"Aye, aye, cap."

We went down and the static lights merged into a steady stream of cosmic artifice. This guy didn't seem so bad after all, but did I want to beat him in some fantastical world, fuck yes. Did I see how that could be the case, sort of but in a very farfetched plausibility. Letting bygones be just that was a tough pill for me to swallow. Regardless, it wasn't my choice, and sticking around for the grand prize seemed like a pathetic gander if I could get out of my own head and spot myself committing the foolish act of desperation.

Around the first sight of the Flatiron Building, Charlie told me we best go back west, and so I ventured down 23rd Street and made a roundabout to where we started at Chelsea Piers. I didn't want to feel paranoid but hell, my association with this guy looked awfully personal, riding around the most monitored city in the world, late night, cavorting in an Aston Martin, after a record breaking unprecedented initial public offering on an internationally traded capital market, and concurrently, being marked in a database every city block on account of the camera installation I could only thank the government for. But I put all this behind me at the time; I was too curious for safety.

I felt like there was a chase, to what, I couldn't wrap my head around, but the future felt like it was there for the taking, all this mishmash of pertinent information, superfluous information posing and doing a good job at posing as pertinent, and the conception of a righteous order to be put together into a structured format for my benefit. But where did Dynamo lurk in the shadows?

Were there spies, operative Dohltrey look-alikes here and now? Then assumption cooled in my mind, but I continued onward to the yacht. The masquerade fit in with what had happened earlier. There were cameras, and I was locked in, sucked in to the mix. Whether it was my own doing, it was relative. I went down to a bottom deck and was surprised that the majority of the rooms were not occupied by sexual deviants and swinging sort of folk. There were only two rooms that fit that bill based on auditory observation. But I frolicked on a couch in a large living room and awaited the suits to quit their squabbling in the office room with Charlie. I heard a few things. Sounded as inside as one could get.

Political swayings, contracts, agreements, options for the future. The news media complex as a tool. What have you, what have you not. Permits were in place. I remained in haphazard darkness. Felt lecherous on account of my ignorance. I sought distraction. Rather than leave, Charlie called me in upon my ascent from the sitting position. He had known I was there the whole time, that I was sure of. Despite my inebriation, there was more to be said and judged.

He introduced me to some mediocre faces but they still commanded authoritative charm, cigars, Cartier watches, and pristine coiffures. I wasn't sure if it was just the superficial sentiment that convinced me but upon their speech, my sentiments were confirmed that they were of acceptable player status in the financial sphere. Whatever that entails, I was and am still not quite sure. But the unknown was a temptation. The youngest one, Aaron, volleyed a question at me. They knew I was a sleuth. He said, "If a guy won't do me a favor, and I keep offering him more and more reward and keep taking on more and more of the risk, what do I do? I'm backed into a corner, and I hate it. It eats at me. I feel like I'm the butt of the joke."

"Confrontation and violence. Man is a foul creature."

"Elaborate, do so, please."

"No matter how flimsy the fella, he's still a man, and he has a primordial instinct somewhere, deep, dark, and buried that's just dying to be freed. Think of a Titan in chains or Atlas under the Earth, you follow?" I said.

Nods.

"In today's mindfully numb, comfortable times, the predisposition for violence is consciously dormant. But, if you present an opportunity for violence to be a healthy option, the opponent has an urge. And this is the key. You present a call to action, a challenge, a duel quote on quote, but no really, but in any case, the option for violence is there. And with that, there's a rush, an instinctual one, as I said. So, you confront, things come to a head, and then you being the one wielding the situation in your favor, back down, swallow what pride you've got left, and let him decide the outcome. Only you already know the outcome is compromise, and if you play your violence in the cards, you've already won, because the compromise will lean in your favor. And now, what do you have?"

"Exactly what I want."

"And more, you have a friend. A collaborator. Better than say, a conspirator, you have an ally, someone to be counted on."

"There's no guarantee."

"Maybe not on the surface, but deep down, you've reached a place where most men dare not venture or care to glimpse."

"But I didn't do anything violent, per se."

"That's just what you seek to believe," I said. "But, in essence, the possibility of its occurrence hitched on your man's choice in the matter makes it one and the same. You see, you gave him the power, and once that exchange happens for even a second, you have made him yours. You challenge, he has some blood boil, a fist squeezed, and then you play the patsy and back down, and cave, and he shows you mercy, in his mind, and you get what you want. And he feels like you respect him, because you put the ball in his court, and he proved he was a worthy opponent by backing down from the fight, following your lead, not that he will probably see that in the most articulate of forms. It's primordial. Trust me."

They nodded, the observers, in utmost pleasure. I was in.

"Ill give you the benefit of the doubt."

"My name's Jean. You know how to get in touch with me."

Brubaker handed the fella a card—It was swell.

Aaron couldn't accept it, wholeheartedly. "So what about the money?"

"That's not a moot point, but it's a less critical one. The way you framed it, that's more of a cherry or icing on the cake. It's not the core backbone. Not with egos. Especially egos with power or money in the first place. Act a role. Act tough, act persistent, act like you won't back down, create the arena for battle, and once he is compelled to answer the call, show signs, hint at signs of respect, of backing down and you've won the war. Let him win the surface battle. C'mon, man, the long view."

The point was made. And Charlie made us all drinks. Brave Bulls, pick me ups because the talk had been too serious for too long. I kept my mouth shut because I never preferred an introduction via diatribe, especially landing in an unfamiliar venue. They proposed cards, but a few of them, including me, shot down the idea, too many tight dresses getting loose on the main deck. Bros will be bros. The jet skis were about to come out, and the captain of the ship had made prior arrangements with the local law enforcement, so it was claimed and communicated via these guys. Wetsuits on, we had a blast, I felt uncomfortable but the active nature of danger has a way of sobering me up. The waves were nonexistent, and I had to rely on my extrasensory instincts because it was rather dark despite the sky high city lights. The horde watched from the deck, and Brubaker was the most impressive, I have to admit. Now, it may sound absurd but there were daftly arranged found objects near the buoys, and I took a leap over and caught air before submerging underwater and going black though the jet ski naturally floated upward. From the applause, it hit the right marks. I thought of making a run to Jersey, but it was quickly shot down when some Coast Guard lights spotlit us cold, low, wet. We followed Charlie's lead and picked up the pace. I enjoyed the jet ski rush, like being on a horse standing, the breaks in the microwaves like the uneven beat of the hooves on the ground. A steady hoofing pace superimposed onto a hybrid motorcycle luge. If this were a wave runner, it'd be even a better comparison. The captain on the boat, named Desiree, flared two great green beams into the sky and the Coast Guards remained with the spotlights, but not for enforcement purpose. They were there to be entertained, and man, now I really got a taste of some rich lifestyle, where the law happens to be a guideline rather than a brick wall hoisted and manned by guns and chains. To be honest, I stopped thinking for the remainder and just enjoyed being a kid again in some dream made real. I took Bree, made sure that was her name, and had a righteous night. Harley did not care.

Just to make things up to speed, there were spies on the boat, and Dynamo now knew my whereabouts and assumed my intentions going forward. At the time, I remained ambivalent of where this could lead me.

I did not even mention Vittoria yet. Don't think I forgot about her and the impending presence she swayed over the course of my actions. I am just plain ole frank about the subject. She was drifting, smiling, looking innocent abroad at the gallery-hybrid-speakeasy spot we had all gone to, but from that point onward, she got lost to my sight. Not that I was making an effort to pay her due attention. Rather, as aforementioned, I was coping the best way I knew how—ignoring, failing to observe—via drink and the casual copulations of our meaning laden society. Harley certainly was a personage cum de coping mechanism. To be denying her superior superficial qualities would be blasphemous on all counts. Such a claim would immediately entail a discomforting accosting of one's person followed by a banishment of opinion privilege and maybe the chopping off of a tongue. Better yet, some teeth would be knocked out or pushed in down the main esophageal tube.

But the eye test goes out the door when feelings are awry. And awry they fully had been, not quite dormant, moreso comatose, only to be jolted with bludgeoning electroshock at a flesh on flesh encounter. Even a pressing thought mentioning the name could debilitate me into some dreadful hopeless state. But I am admitting to the fact that I was still under her spell, nothing more, something less, but my melodrama blows it out of proportion. Regardless, I didn't spot her on the causeway of the boat when we were on the water, waves disturbing the peace that back and forth calm waters exhibit. Maybe I would have been compelled to impress and try to circumvent Charlie's deft abilities. Either way, what was done and what was to come would be a message left at the concierge downstairs for me to do her a common favor at an uncommon time.

The note read, "All this chaos has gotten me stuck up. Charlie took a helicopter to some meeting, and who knows when he'll pop back up. How about a ride in that Aston I spotted you got? I'm lunching at the Minerva with some familiar faces. Please do stop by, babe. Much love and warmth, Vittoria."—Signpost, 11:30 A.M.

It made me feel good that she saw me and wanted my company. Honestly, I planned to be halfway gentlemanly to Bree, but this new scenario cancelled out any preconceived obligation to her. I gave her fifty bucks to get out of dodge and made the most of my time, lollygagging, showering, shitting, smoking, reading the *Journal*, and stopping by the museum to ensure a late arrival.

Even if I couldn't have her in any shape or form or scenario, I could do a solid and look out for her best interests and meet a few dames of quality at the same time. If only her sister had come along, God that could have been some fun. And I am not strictly speaking of a possible sexual tryst.

Feeling foolish was not a strong enough feeling to scare me off. I still willingly went and underwent self-emasculation. How could I not help myself . . . the glitter of posh. God, shame. The company was visible from the street window and lots of blurry half-silhouettes crossed the focal point of their table. It would have been smarter to just fall into line and continue up or down the street and forget about the thing. But being locked in to a fantasy is just as destructive as avoidance or the flight to forget. So I tackled head on, smooth operation to the most subtle of efforts to make believe I had some control. They made room for me in the booth. I was the only male. This was not intimidating but rather exhilarating, mixed with a twinge of disgust. One truth when you have an Athenian conception of a woman, all others diminish in her presence. Kathy worked in advertising, wore a power suit with one of those overtly thick high brim leather belts equipped with one of those obnoxious buckles, hair wrapped in a bun with what looked like chopsticks poking about; Mary, a psychologist version of a mature Alice in Wonderland disposition, slightly red cheeks and a wholesome comfort in a raggy Shakespearian dramatic dress; and then Anna, a photographer who resembled a schoolteacher, in a good way. Except Anna, they could all have met working the club circuit, and I would not have thought any more and especially any less of them. When we got up to go, I took note that none of the ladies had heels on and that made them more endearing, down to earth. Less strain than average in these metropolitan parts. I could kid myself for only so long. Offering rides was a formality that hubris made so. They had affairs to see to. Overall, it was warm and gay.

Vittoria and I walked a couple blocks, got some coffee, and sat by a park area. She laughed at my expense.

"This your idea of a good time?"

"Oh, it's swell. I feel like I'm out for thrills."

"Are you ever not?"

"That is a matter of perspective."

And we kept going, straight ahead.

"So what's your angle?"

"Come again?"

"You got me out here, out of my comfort zone, and seek companionship to some undisclosed destination. I'm just saying . . ."

"Well, that depends on how honest you would like it to be."

"Honest as death."

"Death, eh. Okie."

". . .You should be so cruel."

Some college kids recognized her and they asked if I could take a group photo with one of their phones. I complied.

The conversation's flare had stopped short. Fragmented, it never really started up again the way at the pace it had been going. Out of my control. The way it had happened, Brubaker had started the work week in a torrid disposition to ensure the operations were running smoothly as possible. This was not anything out of the ordinary. From Vittoria's account, he had an insatiable hunger for business, and his acumen resulted in spoils for his whole lot and whoever came into collusion with his beneficiaries. She winked and twirled her hair as she implied that I might see some sunnier paths and lusher clusters of opportunity ahead, and I simply could not even anticipate it yet. This sentiment bothered me, which she knew or suspected, but I did my best to conceal the irritation. By the time she told me her responsibilities for the day and how I could fit in via assistance slash security, we had exited the park and were close to Mickey's on the street bordering south. Vittoria insisted we take a cab to the financial district for her to acquire some valuable intel for Charlie, and we would sweep back around for my car before I took her to the Hamptons—so was the plan. About then, I wondered what Harley could be getting into and how that would be a better bet for me to take advantage of time and place for hedonistic whims.

It sounded iffy. Vittoria was not even in the mix as far as knowledge or context and background information she could gather. I did not call the bullshit but I probably should have. It was around 3:30 then, and we hailed a cab and didn't really talk when we traversed down towards Broad Street. She took the seat behind the driver, and I took the seat behind shotgun and from our positions, we each focused through our respective looking glasses to glimpse at the scenery beside us. We only hit traffic twice, once the midtown Fifth Avenue ruckus and once at the Houston Street juncture. It's amazing the security blanket the barriers of metal and glass convey to the rider. No feelings of smothering or helplessness in the face of mass legions of anonymous pedestrians scooting free in clear, visible sight at a traffic jam. Myriad pedestrians going beside you, arms length—if the windows open and they sneeze when they pass, it would get on you—and others going back and forth. The possibility for danger seemed infinite in scope, yet the safety conjured by the car, on a road that can in essence can open up at a moment's notice, negated the threat of danger.

There was enough sound to go around, and Vittoria was always a silent passenger, one of her most peaceful qualities put into practice. It certainly aided the experience that the cabbie, given name Mohammed Akhbat, had the classical music station on a solid volume with no intention of changing it or altering its strength during the ride. I was in support. Vittoria nudged my shoulder when we cleared Houston Street, and in her hand was a spiral of Fruit Gummis, tautly chewed English candies. These had helped her cope with oral fixations when she decided she should be smoking less. I just enjoyed the taste and thought, *What a rare treat.* The melody on the radio was more akin to a Hans Zimmer or Max Steiner score than a composer of antiquity when we got to the destination just south of city hall and not quite within the financial district's borders. She told me it'd be best for me to wait in the taxi and that she would be back before I could finish my cigarette. She had her mind set on how it was to go down, and I didn't care to argue. Hell, I was still trying my hardest to quit overanalyzing the situation between me and her, so I focused on her behind that she did her best to hide in those clothes as she glided smaller and smaller into the distance down the block before turning a corner into the direction of the park bordering city hall. Mohammed and I made eye contact as she turned away, and he smiled an insipid, insinuating kind of smile, and I grinned back at him. Never take away a man's fantasy; it helps him get through the day, especially with positive reinforcement. Before I lit up on the sidewalk, he offered an exchange with one of his foreign kinds, and it was a respectable arrangement. I could have just smoked in the car, he said, and I told him I did not want to impose. How was I to anticipate that anyhow? He just said he felt I was okay. We were silent as the rest of the time passed. She came back as I stomped mine into the gutter and did not look like anything had happened to her.

As we loaded back into the backseat, I considered that maybe I had botched my duty to snoop and should have perhaps kept an eye on what she was doing. The conflicts of interest mounted in my logical brain, but I quickly shot them down because what more could I consider? When it came to this one, I would always have mistaken my trust and pure perception of her regardless of the evidence so it was a moot point. Missed chances were missed. She had put her handbag on the middle portion of the bench between me and her. There was no attempt to conceal the new object poking out the side : a large, 11" x 15" manila envelope. I made a jab. "Is it normal for a business to ask his girl for clean laundry?" —She gave me a snide look, head tilted down, and finished with a smile to make up for the world and my attitude towards it.

We took a long slow route through SoHo, and by this time, the traffic had accumulated to a disgusting degree. The car ride back uptown did not get off to the magic start that the one downtown had had. Even though we were just as silent as before, the surroundings didn't allow for it to feel as good. Also, there was a commercial break in the radio hymnals, and that advertising can kill any mood. On Prince Street and West Broadway, Vittoria got flabbergasted all of a sudden, apologized for me to forgive her imminent vanishing, and pecked me on the cheek to cool my jets. Strategic dame, I tell you. She bee-lined down the sidewalk after giving me a century bill for the taxi that I didn't want, and she got too far away for me to yell at her to remember to take her bag. I knew she had done that on purpose. High and dry but at least I was sitting. Down the way west, she was in an intense embrace with a long legged, skinny frame with coconut-colored curly hair. That's all I could see. Mohammed sighed to himself and asked how I'd like it. I told him to drive up a block and drop me off, and he did. This handbag really got on my nerves, responsibility now invested in me. It was not because it made me look soft. In actuality, the handbag could be connoted as an extremely stylish man purse, but I still thought it was more acceptable for a gay fashion designer than me. Simply and plainly, I despised carrying around excess weight, especially out of reach of my car, which often served as a mobile locker that could be planted at convenient safe spots. All in all, the assumption of my handling the handbag would be that it was a surety I'd reconvene with Vittoria at a later time that day. A woman's purse contains her life. That still did not make me feel any better. The comfort factor was eliminated and oh well, I fumbled about as the office types emerged from said offices, and so I sauntered to the eastside to ruminate. Nothing worth mentioning. I got a croissant at a posh café and went back down to Canal Street to one of those diners that's not only out of style, they're out of existence in today's world. To be specific, it was a hole in the wall, counter stools, same menu in perpetuity, and the old city guy poured me coffee without asking through words. I loved this vibe, even if Chinatown had taken over all around it and made it seem foreign when it was just the opposite.

I thought about the envelope and its unknown contents, but at that time and place, it made me feel disgusting to be a material voyeur, especially when it came to Vittoria's goods. Sure, I could justify it to myself, if I went through with it, make myself into the white knight, no, the black knight willing to bypass notions of privacy and integrity to get to the bottom of this, this being the interworkings of the Vitti Brubaker potion and unveil how Dynamo had such a keen interest in its possible silver lining. Silver looked fake from here in my denial. But with Dynamo, it must have been platinum. I spotted a couple airline bottles of Jack Daniel's in an inner pocket unzipped and took a full one for myself to give the coffee a necessary punch. The club sandwich was in front of me within five minutes, and it silenced my thoughts for a while. I recall a family of German tourists on my right side and some kids that looked stoned on my left. It rained for the remainder of my meal and by the time I was finished, the streets were glossed over in a lazy semblance of cleanliness. In essence, the light struck the wet just right so details were diminished. Vittoria remained lost in the flux, so I went east down Canal south by the busport block on Allen Street and waded through the traffic and parked cars until I found myself on East Broadway.

The bar east of Rutgers, where Essex Street ends, is called 169, that's the price of a commoditized bottle of water, coincidentally. The water was free there, in glass white coolers with plastic cups stacked in columns messily gathered around the coolers, one third and two thirds down the counter. There was a decadent Southern theme about the place, only neon or fluorescent lights, mirrors everywhere there wasn't brick on the wall, and lava lamps and kitsch paintings of glamour girls wading in the moonlight with a cocktail of someone's choosing. The three-dollar shot and beer deal for happy hour was an alcoholic's wet dream, even if the liquor was watered down to mucus membranous medicinal viscosity. In the shopping mall of Manhattan, a place like this gets older and more desirable, for the sole reason it doesn't care for your business. At least that's the attractiveness that the facade goes for. Low ceilings, '60s Southern soul ballads, and the leopard skin pool table were enough, not to mention the Tyrannosaurus rex bust poking over the sedate fireplace. This rather tall Puerto Rican came in the still rather quiet place, prior to the end of the happy hour rush, and he skipped the pool table to use the bathroom. He left the door open, and I observed his taking of two handfuls of paper towels into his coat pockets before exiting the premises. But then, he came back in and challenged me to a duel, in a loud voice. It sounded like a parody of one of those totalitarian generals in a Western flick centered in conflict around the Mexican revolution.

He broke and the ball flew off the table and landed after ground-spinning, in a corner by the door labeled DO NOT ENTER. I ran the table until I only had the purple four left other than the eight ball, and he proceeded to catch up, with some taunts about leaving the table open for him to clean up along the way. He berated me to get on with it after he missed, and I had peeked at the phone vibrating on my chest in my coat pocket. I didn't respond to the vibration with type so I could have had my way with the game. I made the eight ball off the rail and banked it to the left opposite corner and he accepted defeat with bravado. "Well, guy, you never know."—A spit microball caught the side of my cheek, but I still smiled and struck hands because it seemed like the right thing to do. I felt like having bar food and the Southern accents on the place went as deep as the grill. Po boy, chicken, and sauces for days. I took a seat by the counter by the second cooler, serving as a block from the guy that was on the end of the bar. He kept giving me these weird glances, not quite stares, and the way he looked overall was wrong. Medium height, junkie thin, Nascar nylon racing coat, and eyes like a rat's, with pupils too big and black. The cooler temporarily relieved me of my worry.

On the television was an old movie, Golden Girls era aesthetic, with glossy plastic gilded guns and chicks in high boots with bikinis on a beach. Hell, now that I can recall, it could have been a James Bond knock-off.

I was eight drinks deep by the time the food came out, four shots, four beers. The patio in the back was chained shut so I had to smoke out front and spectate as the worker bees came home and the Seward Park chillers vegetated across the street. The sun was descending cinema-like to the west peek-a-booing between the trio of buildings in the background situated up and triangulated due to the road delta. You see, the road East Broadway crossed west-east, but if going to Canal, a right lane veered north slightly and the streets converged on the right lane serving as a hypotenuse, with Essex slash Rutgers being the base for the right angle. Maybe Five Points used to be like this, the clear openings in an urban environment without any digital lights and ad posters denaturalizing the beauty of masonry and architecture. Snoopy racer came outside for a smoke as I reentered to commence consumption, and I hoped he would just go away to the hole whence he sprang.

I got particularly sloppy with the chicken. There was an oldie on, "Ain't no mountain high, ain't no valley low, ain't no river wide enough, baby, if you need me, call me, no matter where you are . . ." when I viciously chomped away, mixing all the sauces into a concoction of molasses like ooze. My fingers changed color on account of the mess and I assumed so did my lips. Lucky, upon further inspection in the ladies' bathroom (the men's had no mirror), there was no spillage on the clothing. When I emerged, I reclaimed my stool and got caught up with James Coburn on the screen crashing a utopian island paradise destination by jacking a guard's uniform. I finished my Pabst and under the can when I put it down, I noticed a card, white that had a black dot on it . . . Dynamo. I didn't panic, but I did scan the room smooth and suave and slow, glancing about the mirrors. Then I took myself out for a smoke break. It was getting more crowded now, the closing bell for happy hour's end imminent until the next day's cycle, so it was hard for me to determine my standing. But the creeper from before was still where he had been, and I had the inclination he was keeping pervasive eyes on my comings and goings. I was visibly buzzed, eyes slightly red, my face relaxed.

My buzz mounted into a hyper drunk, but I could still judge all right. At about 7:27, the beer can in front of me was empty, and the voices were loud and wailing in merriment crossed with mimicries of merriment. The masks of ruckus were full fledged all around, and it felt chaotic but controlled. The front door had a jerking hinge and it kept going open and closed, users in and out at a galloping pace. Coburn, by then, had descended off the screen and De Niro in *Cape Fear* had brought his menacing gaze to the ill-attentive spectators. It was about time and with my paranoia ready, I assumed beady eyes would follow my lead. He did, he actually held the door open for me as we got out on East Broadway. I asked for a light, and he gave it, and we proceeded as if there was an understanding already. He suggested we walk through the park, and I jockeyed, "So you can kill me without any witnesses . . ." He looked smug but cheeky. When we got to the park area by the library clearing in the front with the big oaks, I handed him the card with the black hole—"Think you lost something . . ."

"Just a way to reel you in. I'm not your average stalker."

"Sure."

"Let's get this straight. The name's Bobby, Dean, Bobby Dean, and you're my responsibility."

"In your jurisdiction?"

"You could say. That's a matter of formalities."

"How you figure?"

"What's that supposed to mean?"

"Nothing."

"You're a pesky guy."

"Shouldn't you be taking notes or something?"

"Don't get cute, sleuth, assume anything you've got to hide has already been found."

"Just 'cause it may be found doesn't mean it may be used."

"In any case, you're overstepping some boundaries."

"Do you consider me a threat?"

"Ha, threat . . . no, more a nuisance."

"If I'm wasting your time, you're free to go."

"Give me a cigarette."

"Will you get on?"

"Well won't you find out after you hand it over . . ."

"So be it."—I lit up another for myself. We were getting near the end of the park, and so we walked on the blacktops with the hoops and handball courts. It was about nighttime now.

"So, I get it, you're a slick operator, you're in with the sort of *in* crowd, and you think you're untouchable. Self righteous self deception."

"Get to something substantive."

"If you would shut your trap, maybe this could get over with."

"You're just gonna check up on me, have me followed."

"So you accept defeat."

"I didn't say that."

"You accept you can't get out free."

"Hey, I'm already in. Why would I get out, now?"

He smirked and chuckled like a girl was fiddling with his pinky toe. It was self-deprecating, but he didn't seem to care.

"You probably already know too much, and I'm gonna stick by that assumption." He kept eyeing the handbag in the plastic bag. I waited for him to get to some sort of point. ". . . You're a walking liability and so, my job is to get you gone, gone now, gone for good."

"How do you make out you're gonna do that?"

We stopped walking and stayed in the middle of the blacktop courts.

"You already took the money and ran once. So I've taken the liberty to get creative."—He pulled out an envelope. I opened it. Two tickets to my destination of choice, worldwide, Lufthansa, first class. Not bad. I giggled. I wasn't sure if I was laughing at the attempt at creativity or just 'cause I was plain pleased it wasn't.

"But that's enough, I know, I've studied you, you're a two face."

"I'm all ears."

"Why do you think you're at where you're at?"

"Don't pigeonhole me into telling you any more."

"You don't find it funny that you got into this for a menial task, and that coincidence just so happens to curtail you into a bind of inter-weaving developments . . ."

"May be more illustrious than a typical deal, but whose to say what. I'm no judge."

"Consider me one. Don't trust me but heed my words. You're in over your head. There are ideologies and institutions that enforce these and can come down unto you, and when you realize, it will be beyond me to help."

"I already said, Why would I get out?"

"Quit trying to frustrate me because I refuse to budge. This is what it is."

"You keep on the way you keep, and I'll do the same. Just do your job and stay out of my way."

"That is not the way it works, Jean-O. Ultimatum: Two days, scram the city, and whatever you do, restrain yourself from the royal couple. They'll be your demise."

I didn't pester him for who had what to lose, I wasn't listening. Bobby Dean, the messenger of the gods in a semi-free world. He didn't try to say any more except, "Keep that card—You find yourself in and it's too deep, you can get out."

"Fuck off and die," would have been the best salutation. When I exited the blacktop and reached the street corner of Grand and Essex, I glanced back, and he was nowhere to be found. Vanished to a point. It was darker, I guess. Harley called me, and I ignored it. Vittoria, I answered. What was on my mind was this impending inconvenience growing more inconvenient by the passing of time in the form of a crunchy getting more distorted black plastic bag containing the keys to her existence. But I kept that to myself. Her voice was perfect for any naughty thought so I just hummed and shuffled and nodded my head while I distracted myself with the burgeoning city lights. I responded with a couple yeahs, a few no's, and a maybe, and by then, we had decided to meet at the hotel. I'd pick up the car on the way. Yada yada yada. Fortune was playing a trick on me, I had a nefarious inkling to excrete waste, rectally. I still finished my cigarette because tobacco could never go to waste. There wasn't time to track down a cab, so I loaded into a livery car and was back at the Warwick before I could count to one hundred. The download was rampant after an initial tussle, struggle the flood-gates opened and so did a good-riddance shower. No shame, just biological necessity. I still had enough time to fetch the car I thought so I went about it at a leisurely pace.

You lose track of the date in the city, bloodhounds of both sexes scouring and looting for their opposites in the banter of consumption once the night lights brighten up the place. I admit it was entertaining for the voyeur. Such variation, myriad combinations of mutant human proportions. Freaks, all of them, and I was glad to be one of them in what was left of my waning stupor. Coffee fixed and maintained my strength for whatever might come. By the time the car was around my body, it had worn off. The door guy at the hotel kept it out front, and I fetched the bag from my room because I felt safer keeping it up there rather than in the hands of the front desk clerk. The concierge was off by this time. I messaged Vittoria I'd be around the block so to just tell me her whereabouts and I'd swoop her to get her off her feet and onto her ass beside me, in many fewer words than that. But before that, the front desk guy named Noah handed me a note on my way out. It was from Rex. It was in all caps. Livid cannot begin to describe it so here it is verbatim,

MAN, WHY YOU PLAYING ME
LIKE THIS? THIS IS GREENLIT, WE —
NEED TO GO NOW, AND OUT
OF ALL THINGS, YOU SCURRY OFF TO —
CITY FUCKING COME. BUST
YOUR ASS BACK HERE, PRONTO, THERE'S —
TICKET WAITING FOR
YOU AT THE JFK DELTA TERMINAL —
CONCIERGE. DEAR MOTHER OF
GOD, IT MAY SOUND LIKE I AM —
TOTALLY LOSING IT BUT IN
REALITY, I JUST NEED YOU IN THE —
MEETINGS. AND PLEASE SIGN

SOME DOCUMENTS (E-SIGNATURE) IF —
YOU CHECK YOUR EMAIL.
THANKS. OH, AND TELL CHARLIE TO GO —
FUCK HIMSELF BECAUSE
HE HAD TO GO PUBLIC
THE ONLY WEEK OF —
THE YEAR I COULDN'T
ESCAPE FROM LA. REX

What was going on? Was I actually involved in a Hollywood production? Was everyone batshit crazy, or was I just drunk? I felt like an idiot. All in all though, this car seat was comfortable and the way the steering wheel was situated at the perfect windshield and control panel just had me all right. Enjoying the little moments, however minuscule. Harley called me again and upon ignoring, left a message. The voice wasn't mail as much as it was a Virus or CDC level disease of raucous intensity. She demanded my whereabouts, my participation in her foray into the Hamptons, and an immediate rescue from whatever doom she had set herself up for. To be specific, it was two ex football players named Dino and DeAndre and they were all in for a gangland slaying. Hysterical to me was her hysterical fright. What a boor.

I stared at my eyes caught in the rearview mirror and looked away past them at my skin and brows because I didn't want to face myself. Instead of apathy, they should dub it the "Oh-wells" or the "Sighs." Just speaking for myself, *res ipsa loquitur* was getting old and in an ever perpetual present hallucination, I needed a drink to make the edges soft and dull. Luckily, Vittoria came up to the car without me having to move, and I could relieve myself of feeling isolated in general. She wasn't wearing the same thing, obviously why she took so long, but it was worth it. Not really for me because they were goth-ninja black robes with narrow curtains jagged around her joints and limbs but for her, she surely felt like a secret agent from a medieval tale with specters and goblins. I shared my sentiment, "Going to the castle?"—She rolled her hair back and didn't verbally jab back. We carried on, and the roads opened once we got to the ways high and afar. The waters were reintegrating and disintegrating the moonlight in meager orbital refractions and the transference of crossing a body of water floating in inertia ignored by engine sounds made us at peace, accompanied by road songs from southern American blues, guys with beards we're only cognizant of via voices solemn and true.

I thought about telling her about certain developments in the Dynamo sphere but breaking the silent ice would have been the wrong thing to do. She did, after a row of cigarettes. When we were past the parkways of the city and out to the island, in Jewish country. She recalled an shaved ice stand a bit of a ways off in Hewlett, and I said what the heck. So we broke ice—I got a blueberry, she got a cherry, and continued back onto the causeway in decadence. It was dark fully now, though so you couldn't really tell when we bypassed high and low places, unless you acknowledged the signs and their maintenance or lack thereof. I ignored them and the road with the dotted lines stabilized me. She started, "You're gonna see where I'll be."

"Staying?"

"For the time being."

"Being what?"

"Being the whole rest of the year."

"Glad to know you're looking ahead."

"You should keep Amelie company."

"I will."

"I think he's going to propose to me."

"You sound like you should be more excited."

"But I'm not."

"Because?"

"Because I don't know. I'm just not."

She looked over to me, but I didn't break sight of the road. We were silent for a while.

I was disappointed. Not with what was bound to occur. More so, her response. It was banal, beneath her and the way I considered her. After the silence was overriding and the southern rock cooled into a morose ballad of love lost along the trail of mice and men, I got it in my head that I probably was not the best person to volley back and forth emotional thoughts. She needed a woman's intuition, a woman's mind, and what could I do but commence my duty of silence, strong and dumb, like my balls.

When we finally got there, almost to Montauk, close to the borders, "Knocking on Heaven's Door" by Dylan was playing, and I conned myself into a thought framework as in Peckinpah's film *Pat Garrett and Billy the Kid* dusting in the timeless waste of Western nature with nothing to really say and no way to really communicate anything at all. But that would change quickly when we got to the right street.

11

THE HOUSE looked like a wooden ornament in a Japanese sand garden. It came into full view through my side mirrors because I backed in the straight driveway to make the getaway convenient. I never intended on staying the night. It was too grand of a monstrosity to be captured in the rearview mirror though the bodily movements of shaded figures catapulted forward through the interior lights. When we stepped out to the pavement, the sight was a letdown. Sure, it was aesthetically acceptable, but the minimalist design and success at attempting to merge the estate with the landscape overrode a hint of antiquated luxury. All in all, I expected some sort of Rothschild-Rockefeller mausoleum to aristocratic excess, but I suppose Gatsbyland had permeated the themes of not only West but also Easthampton. There was no loud bass held in by a bubble about to burst and that was nice to my senses, the cool dirge of whispering voices not drained out.

Vittoria turned back with a look like "Get on with yourself, come on in," but I nodded and alluded to the cigarettes in my pocket. I preferred to have to brood on the surprising sight. She didn't wait. I didn't expect her to. Harley kept bumbling notifications via my mobile phone, and I decided to turn it off. There was a courtyard with a Zen sort of fountain, no figurine décor, and the front doors were absent as the courtyard gave way to a lifesize stone arrangement with figs and thorns serving as borders between the wall stones and floor tiles. The foyer was quaintly undersized before it opened to an open air drawing air with three-story-high windows overlooking the north shore. Little heads went side-ways up and down, so I got a picture of where the stairs could be to go down into the deep. I realized I was on the second floor though it was ground when I could not get down from the open air outdoor attachment. It was a bulbous terrace, and the spectacle was in full accord with my imagination. More long dresses, furs, and jewels sparkling in the moonlight than the boat foray. I turned around and got a view of the house's backside, and it looked like it should have been the front side if it were up to me, judging composition and humble obvious wealth. In the east wing bay window above, I saw what looked like blood splatter against it and sauntered through the easy-to-navigate labyrinth up to the room past some Oriental structures and wall lining waterfalls.

The door was open and on the southern wall, I was facing east, so right side, a magnificent sized canvas, twenty feet or so high, hinged on a pulley system pretty deftly constructed. It was not blood then, instead a deep auburn. The perpetrators were rail thin young guns and a dapper fruitcake with a shaved head and parts on both sides of his forehead. Bailey, Laura, Nancy, and Gunnar. What a bunch. Over what had to be undergarments, unless my mind perceived otherwise, Dickies workwear white smothered in a miasma of colorful nicety. When they noticed I had come in, the last thing Gunnar asked them, Was he sporting the Samo look? I considered this a travesty, assuming it had to be Vittoria's workstation getting raped and pillaged by unsavory marauders. In any case, that notion was quickly shot down by my discovery that the house was functioning as a seminal gathering point for artistic types of merit, meaning the type of merit only account balances and shoddy connections can get you to create tax shelters and tentative residences, hence in-house.

Gunnar was the one and they were sort of playing like they would prefer to be his minions in a rainbow manmade Wonderland, two-dimensional of course. They welcomed me to the party on the condition that I did not hold it against them if they happened to brighten up my drab garb. I said, "Hey, this is not even vintage, just worn." And when they guessed brand, Laura was right on the third try, Valentino. Nancy said shucks, but Gunnar came to my defense and noted that timeless is what matters. Maybe they weren't so bad in their facades. It's not like I could even discover more or expect to get to know these people as more than exhibitionists in their own wrongs and rights.

To blow everything out of proportion in scale and scope, Gunnar had delineated the act of chaos to be a byproduct of consequential importance contingent upon spontaneous combustion of sensory inhibitions. Once sedate, free, liberated, the minion models were to alter the canvas, already filled in with a multitude of arrangements that simple and plain were geometric shapes stacked on top of one another as a totem pole, placed beside one another as a man and a woman, abstract in only the most trivial of sentiments. I gathered it was an early Rothko, prior to his triptychs and linear modality and international renown; it turnt out I was the ignoramus; it was a Philip Guston, original, acquired for the sole purpose of antiappropriation. Rather, it was to be, merged with the time space continuum, hence, now the future for the abstract expressionists and augmented by the powers that be, the sole benefactor being Gunnar's sponsor, finally getting around the circles back to Brubaker. I partook in the bong loads but not in the defilement of an image considered part of the historical canon. I had no desire to ransack an image. But the more and more high and aware I became of my close-in-proximity visions, the more had I noticed the overalls they were wearing had nothing but dermis and epidermis underneath and they sure looked appealing.

A couple of heavy stone lamps did not have their shades, as they were hitched on their sides with sheets from the walls hinged and screwed knot by nails, so the lights would diffuse through them. I looked upwards as the ladies stood that way and cavorted in oracular trance motion. Above their heads the windows caught my gaze, and I considered that the room must have an influx of sunlight to the breaking of the barrier. I focused on the red splatter and then an array of yellows reached and crossed over the reds and with my head and gaze adjusting downward, I saw that Bailey was the perpetrator. Smart gal. She suggested, in a Pollockian sense, to emulate his physicality in the makings of his works, we should turn over the dying disintegrating Guston canvas and use the backside as a horizontal plane to construct a subconscious spawn. An ode to the surrealists.

My watch said it was around almost one, and I had an urge to inject more smokes into myself, so I rationalized it out as if it could not be so bad if we happened to not see the defilement. Heck, they were already guilty; it was not as if I could undo what they had done and even if I was to be apt to do so, the canvas was already irreparably damaged. Guston's spirit must have been jaded. But mine transcended. I watched the ladies climb the ladders and sway in ease like trapeze artists, not the clumsy sort of hot but a sportier coordinated kind, like nymphs in a fairy tale. And Bailey jumped down, released the pulley system, and the canvas came slithering down like an avalanche in slow motion. The stone floor of the room would be having a mixer were the canvas still wet. Them damn oils; patience wore thin without defenses. A nip slip came out by Laura and upon noticing it, she undid a strap of her overalls and thus set the chapter for a new circle of smokes. Apparently, they were showing in three separate one-man galleries at the start of the fall, coinciding with the Fashion Week roar so as to leverage their exposure. I thought it was more marginalizing but kept this to myself.

But they claimed they had done their duties politically and were segueing their bodily beauty to more fruitful endeavors. Had to admit, I respected that they did not care to just get married off to any billionaire. It had to be somebody. I think I puked in my mouth when they started to gossip, especially when the managerial force of Gunnar lapsed into participation. Gossip, the start of storms not yet seen for millions of miles. Millions because the earth spins every day and who knows when the time will come before it finally emerges in a hydra-like form of uncontrollable scale and intensity. The melodrama must have leaked into my senses . . . I took a deep breath to make sure it had just been a taste in my mouth, not actual regurgitations.

I heard the faint echo of a cork pop, somewhere out the hallway, and a few milliseconds went by when I got my answer as it struck my right shoulder. The chicks in Indian-style cross-legged poses rebelled forward into predatory positions to snatch the item of interest. As they argued about who could use it, already coated with paint separating from their asses, I looked back from where the throw must have come. There was no one there. I had a couple of ideas of who it could have been, but they were not necessarily important at the time, especially since I needed to get my last rip in before I got on my way and did my sort of apathetic flirting with chicks deluded to distraction. It was a pleasure.

I said my goodbyes with no intent of seeing them again, at least with a preconceived plan, but like a calculating dog, I wanted to know where that bottle the cork popped off of could have come from. Maybe he kept a stash of the best goods in his office rather than the subterranean cellar. I saw at the first two doors on the right side, one was for a closet, the other a guest bedroom. On a whim, I hurled myself at the other end of the hall, past the stairs. There at the end was the room I had sought, a perfect alpha's personal office, equipped with billiard table, plush seating, a fireplace, and a stone counter bar. This was the place where I found some spillage and a lingering cigarette in an ashtray on the mantle. The television—the bottommost one on the wall, as there were four, two by two, so the left bottom one—was mute with a replay of a Premier League soccer game. By their uniforms, it looked like Liverpool was playing somebody. But they all looked the same so I couldn't vouch for that. In any case, the other three screens were colored video cameras, surveying the spectacle below. My car was positioned right in the spot where I had left it, and I beamed my head deep into the screen so the images got more pronounced but less clear when I saw moving parts.

A bottle of wine, it had to be, because it rolled along from where the house was on screen and leaked staining red on the concrete driveway before crashing into my right back tire. I did my best to keep track of where it had come from on the screen, but the other two screens were unrelated in boundary or scope. I found a clicker on the desk and pushed buttons 'til the screens responded. The red stain came up on the right top screen on the courtyard, but from there I did not know where to look. I continued to look. Another shuffling of the images with the remote clicker, and the scene was in full display: It looked like two were playing a game with each other's necks, somewhere in the house, or more specific, around its exterior, in a place I had yet to see.

The voyeur in me was absent of shame, and I lit a cigarette, no, I mean I lit the one that just went out from on the mantle. It was a Parliament, but it didn't have lipstick. In ten seconds or less, I figured out there was a zoom capability on the cameras and a joystick, too. I treated myself to some violation of privacy. There was a rush in it, even if so many denied and condemned the act overall. I situated the viewing plane slightly closer, more in alignment with the moving body parts . . . I just wish I knew where the sound button was. But yeah, ten seconds or so, I switched it to black and white and decided there was more to see in the grain like that.

The chick bit too hard because the guy's mouth came off her neck and there should have been a cry of pain when his mouth opened in a vision of agony. I giggled, c'mon buddy, but judging by the chick's continued action, maybe she was over the top. So, carrying on, he shoved her away. He shook his head and rubbed his bleeding neck and turned to face the camera when I zoomed out and this look of anguish crossed with disbelief collided on his face. I still couldn't get a clear view of the guy's mug, and hence, his identity was still unknown. I could still see his mouth skewed in the shadow. He had to have muttered "what the fuck?" to himself, if I could guess. Either way, he had to be thinking something along those lines. In a sudden change of pace, he turned back, swiveling and swerving the tramp by her hips and slammed her on the concrete house exterior. She stepped on a garden light, and it shattered because it went sort of dark after that. But their upper regions were still visible in a much starker hue. I turned the color back on and pulled back just as her green dress was coming off. She liked the intensity, visibly turning on. She took out a penknife from her purse and cut off the straps from the top of her dress. This was getting freaky. The guy kept on getting himself up and ready by rubbing her hooters despite the presence of the sharp object in her hand. She turned around so her boobs squeezed against the wall and her ass stuck out in an arch, and, at her suggestion, the guy leaned over and took hold of the knife. He put it on her neck, and she curved her head back in the most seductive ecstasy I wish I could see in a serious pornographic drama. Cheese should have seen this glory hole of reality porn, what an innovative concept—Okay, maybe things were just softcore but to put it plainly, it was fully loaded. The shimmer of the blade was barely there on account of the shattered ground light but it shone enough to register when he switched hands and put it around her thigh area, and then I lost sight of what was still left of the dress until he eviscerated a seam in one swooping motion. Dude's veins were pulsating with reckless abandon. In another moment, when penetration was bound to occur, it didn't.

The chick got vicious, biting off his cufflink from his left sleeve and opening her mouth to moan, not scream. It was carnally consensual, and he started doing the business from behind, and she used the wall as leverage to bop back and forth, up and down, diagonally. The foreplay was much more exciting because now I knew what to expect. I went to the mantle and put out the cigarette and came back to get a last peek. I started resetting the zoom and color settings to default when I got scared hellish sober. Rather, my high did not know how to register the sight. He looked as if he was peaking, reaching climax, and thrusting with voracious force, full bodily strain, wrinkles gathering in the botched dress at their hips. His mouth growled open, and he had to have been grinding his teeth. He pulled her hair back, and when he released it, she had her arms wrapped behind his head in a fountain-like pose, and she lost her balance, and her head smashed into the concrete. She went limp. And I don't think he finished inside her. You see, just to be clear and put me in the clear, the view was diagonally from the backside, so I saw some profile but never got a full view. She staggered to the ground, and I'm betting the chap's eyes were closed because he spewed his blood and guts via semen onto her body. It had to be because he stayed poised for some time with his head tilted up, and when it tilted down and his eyes must have opened, the horror made him react. He zipped up, wiped his hair back, looked around, then looked at her, then measured her pulse, then did it again, and then started lifting his arms pacing away from the camera. I sighed to myself, whoa, without the emphasis on the *-oa* and sparked up another, and swigged the bottle of old Scotch because I was getting uncomfortable standing as witness. I felt some kind of responsibility play out of my running interior monologue but waited to see what violator would do. Faceless violator, still caught in the shadows, scrammed, and I took note to switch back to the driveway cameras to see if he was making a run for it. Before I got back to that first set of cameras, I noticed there was a camera within the very room I was standing in and it shone on my backside right where I was. I was afraid of that and seeing my fear made real annoyed me. With a grimace, I switched back to the driveway shots, and he wasn't there. There were no tires, engines running, or lights showing the way out of the darkness. So these cameras didn't showcase the entire house. On the opposite side of the mantle, there were more screens, but they were blank. I volleyed around and flipped a few switches on the desk to get them on and after switching the input—because what do you know, there were Nelly music videos with tits and asses and guns and cars and drills and jewels—I caught sight of the guy going back towards the party.

But no cameras showed where he had gone. There were none of the stairs, and I knew he had to be inside in a blind spot, most likely a bathroom. Heck, I wasn't on duty, but duty is duty. Go to her first or try to teach long john mystery face a lesson . . . the girl was my priority. I found my way there down the stairs and to the west side of the house. There were no signs, it was like a maze of levels and hallways and rooms. I suppose between the courtyard and that hallway, there was a blind spot because it opened into a lawn and about one hundred feet west there was a gazebo guesthouse that could have been a postmodern tomb for a contemporary dead fellow. She was there, and in the same position, and she was dead. I felt awful. I had a thing about dead bodies so I didn't want to touch her and put her in a more respectable position. I did it anyway, but it made me feel like the thing was my fault. The witness dilemma. I laid my coat over her and decided it looked too merciless, so I folded it into a neat small pad and rested her head on it like a pillow. I even made sure her eyes were closed. The knife was still there beside her, and she was bleeding. Is this what I missed on the screen from the backside view? Make it out to look like an actual rape? He did have his handkerchief out, but I didn't rewind the tape. Hell, I couldn't have looked away for more than a couple seconds. Excuses rationalized my stupidity. I left my coat there and went to find Brubaker, because it was my duty and all.

I couldn't find him for a while. I didn't want to tell Vittoria, because she shouldn't have to know right then, that night. Harley told me she was the one who threw the cork and didn't want to talk to me until she got drunker. Neither of them knew where he was. They said to check the dock, and I did, and he wasn't there. When I got back from the dock, Harley nudged me and as if she wasn't still pissed at me, she said she had seen him go up to the house, and who knows where. I went back up to the office, and he must have been in the bathroom because the door was closed and the sink was on. When he came out, I was sitting, facing away from him on the couch, smoking, so I didn't get a look at his face direct. However, the mirror where I could see it reflected didn't tell me much. He looked calm and collected as you can for being a drunk at your own debacle.

I went through the casual talk of getting familiar and saying thanks for welcoming me to his home even if it wasn't through the most proper of channels on account of the debacle, but he seemed like there was nothing oppressing on his mind. He didn't seem too innocent though, just the right amount, offering me some cocaine, goofing on me for opening up the Scotch, and showing me his bonafide maximum security prison type of set up with the cameras. He was glad to see me as a buddy, I guess, grabbing my shoulder with his hand, laughing at some stumbling chicks, and winking at what festivities were to come.

But after the first laugh, I told him to take a look at the right side cameras by the soccer game. It wasn't there, and I quivered in recoil.

We ended up rewinding the tape, but before that—I had him go through the entire shebang, figured it was a digital tour on the premises and what better way to get a glimpse at all of it via the comfort of cameras and cigars. He agreed, and so we went through it and there was no sign of foul play in the scene where the foul play had occurred. After we went through all possible viewpoints, I asked if there were tapes and he said "yes and no," . . . "screw analog" were his exact words, and that the tapes automatically uploaded and backed up to a server in the office, which he revealed under a cupboard of some rare wood nearby. Fullproof? Fullproof, he insisted. I nixed the feeling of the cigar in my mouth and upon returning to my cigarette of choice, screw the Parliaments, I needed a light, I said, because I couldn't seem to find mine at the time. He lit mine up—His cuff link was torn off.

There were no other signs on the surface. We made eye contact after the smoke was aflame, and I nodded in recognition and thanks. The whole crime could have not been committed and cleaned up within the last ten minutes, so instead of running through the digital mainframe, I asked him about the place, and he revealed its history and architecture with no hesitations. The gazebo guesthouse was originally intended to be a place for meditation, ceremony, or the creation of art. He assumed I had already guessed the original builder and owner of the estate was a former fashion designer specifically transformed into an artist, visual, installation, isolationist. Charlie admitted he basically left the place intact, the way it was meant to be, studio upstairs, studio downstairs, and only the gazebo guesthouse altered to contain a bedroom, bathroom, and the dock spruced up for appearances. We poured full glasses of Scotch and went on our way. On the walk through the courtyard, he revealed he had an affinity for the arts that went back to his schooling years, that no matter his desire or inclination, the arts seemed to him a mystical harbinger of human expressions that numbers and suits could never fully encompass. Artists were on to something and whether it be familial obligations or sheer consideration of logic in a money marked environment, he would never get to explore or discover until after the financial track had run its course to reach a place where he had security. Now, the time had finally come, and somewhat precipitated by his relationships with women, relationships that stimulated his dormant desires for abstraction and emotional cultivation, hence, art. Charlie really enjoyed hearing himself speak, and was it not for the coke, I probably would have been left much further in the dark about desire and that obscure object of his.

After a request to get a picture of the place, he turned up the lights and it was impeccably clean, wiped down, no signs. As we walked down the corridor, which was where the perpetrator had fled, I noticed a long streak of hair, had to be a woman's, poking out from the rocky borders of the walkway. I made a note of it. And we went around, and he showed me where I only could have previously imagined the perpetrator had fled to freedom. The grasses sloped down beside the house and one could bypass the terrace stairs from the ground floor to reach where we walked and talked to get to dock level. We were both silent by the beat of the low tide and he said, "I need to get out more." I said, "I'm out now." Then he looked at me and paused before responding, "Really." We shared a laugh. Before we reached the congregation at the actual dock, I couldn't help myself and asked, "Why the torn cuff?" He looked at it with an aghast expression, sighed, "That damn dog—" Then I heard a bark from an upstairs room, and he said he would see to it—I was played out. But there was that streak of hair and maybe some evidence could begin to unfold. I hoped, but not too much.

A few moments after refilling the glass of Scotch, I was surely inebriated. The stoned feeling pretty much wore off, but I felt foolish on all fronts. Harley's company was a relief. Then the reflection of sirens carried through the front of the estate through the glass windows to the back, and they almost looked like works of fire.

The cops were there, out front, and the congregation followed, quiet, whispers and concerns. When we made our way up the stairs to ground level and got inside, there was a stretcher going upstairs. When it came down, there was a girl on a respirator, had to be the one that was on the screen before, but her dress was different. I looked to see if Vittoria was there, and if her expression would change if the dress happened to be hers. She wasn't around. I had nothing. Out of all the attendees, it appeared that the overdose victim had come on her own, and that she had only loose ties to the bunch. The sirens all went away, and the party resumed.

The newspaper the following morning had an article dedicated to her demise, her name was Nico Fabrizi and she had been on the ballet circuit and now was no more. Brubaker's name was mentioned as the sight of the tragedy—I ended up staying the night because I wanted to see the reaction from the morning. Harley shook her head, as did Vittoria, and Brubaker read it, and retreated to his office for a consultation. He asked me along. The same faces from the boat party, absent Aaron, were present, in bathrobes. There would be a backlash, this much we all could be sure about, but the ramifications of such a backlash could be controlled, point being, saving face, reputations, and all that.

With death, scandal comes next. To mitigate the hellacious risk of money potentially lost from such a backlash, they had to act quickly. The two oldest guys waited for us to quibble and agree and argue and play advocates to devils and gods, turning into each other within blinkings of eyes and sighs of angst. They said in unison, "Damage control—" then, "we need a patsy." They stared at Charlie. He was offended, his eyes bulged out in disbelief, but I filled him in with what they had said in so few words: "You're the leader, this is your property, hence, you're responsible. Therefore, you come out first, express your condolences, and volunteer all the help you can give to determine who was the culprit of the drugs-sex offense."

He said, after scratching his chin, "One of these artists would crave this sort of publicity—" We all laughed, not because it was a ludicrous claim but because such a ludicrous claim held water and could be the best outcome for all. Stupidity breeds simplicity, which spawned a miracle. That's how he looked. I said I had just the right guy, went and fetched Gunnar, passed out in the room. I had last seen him the night before. I brought him in. Charlie kicked everyone out, including me, with the exception of the two old guys in robes, and before the door shut, I heard Gunnar's fruity voice—"How much?"—and "Is there any jail time involved?"

12

I DIDN'T want to say goodbye to Vittoria, and I didn't. I was all torn up. Harley kept herself sounding ignorant. I had no reason to suspect otherwise. My gut kept telling me to keep my mouth shut and just let it play out the way they wanted it to, and come a few weeks, or months down the path, my memory would quit reminding me of all the dirty details. The next day's paper gave me the answer—Charlie admitted he was a deviant involved in the consumption of pharmaceutical drugs, cannabis, and hallucinogenics, and that after such an instance, when he was seemingly on the road to unsurpassed riches, he had faltered, not to himself, but to the others around him, and such a focal event required him to commit himself to a rehabilitation institute. He would be stepping down from his position as Chairman and Chief Executive Officer of Brubaker Air, indefinitely, and this precedence for such a company should illustrate the commitment to excellence the company is obligated to provide for its shareholders. The stock price rose 20 percent the next day, and I was on a plane back to Los Angeles.

The day of my flight, the article of interest focused on Gunnar, who took the blame for providing the drugs, intended for personal use, as he got to showcase his artistry and benefactor association with Brubaker while expressing his sincerest apologies for the death. In closing, his next show was to showcase three women of fine disposition, similar in age and background to Nico, and that this showcase would be dedicated to her memory, with certain proceeds going to charity via a fundraiser. Bailey, Laura, and Nancy were in a spread in the Arts section. When I got home, I wanted to forget about it all. The dude Charlie was on some higher level of operation, untouchable. Hell, the way I seen it, he wasn't untouchable, he couldn't be, because he was beyond reach, he was off the pecking order. That wasn't really the concern at the forefront of what was left on my mind. It was more how Vittoria had been reeled in to the shade never to return. The cave was fortified, and she had a suite. So be it.

When I awoke from my slumber, I felt better because I was back on western time. As dumb as that sounds, it made a difference. I had a message from Rex on my hardline answering machine, sarcastic remarks thanking me for forms I had yet to sign, but really, I should come to the studio tomorrow and get it all done, now that he knew I was in Los Angeles. To hell with it; I didn't want to think about it.

There was another message from Vittoria. She sounded all wrought up in wrongs, felt left out to dry, and was coming back to California, where she could run back to safe harbor. All in all, she needed a ride. Her sister was preoccupied. Noon tomorrow, the commitments kept piling up.

The sunlight still held on to the day, probably for another two hours, so I buckled up and rode over to Hel's lot. Loved the feeling of being back on familiar pavement, with a familiar steering wheel, and a seat and mirrors that did not need adjusting. Like it was waiting for me to purr the engine onward and slick the pavement behind me gathering dust. The Jaguar was in tip top shape, the way I had it figured before, was we could plant a bug from a gadget from some guy I knew, coincidentally through Rollins, and just keep tabs on Moser, especially if he happened to harass Hel in the imminent meet ahead. Now, the way I saw it, better for me to just deliver the car, cut the crap, get a view of the facilities at Open Doors, and based on what transpired with Brubaker in the eastern ward, I doubted any hell would break loose.

Hel said something with conviction, unexpected, but he had a way with articulation, and when he wasn't shitting himself, it shone through. He demanded to accompany me, or rather, that I accompany him. No solo missions. This was still a business transaction, and he still sought to maintain his rep and get the green addition to his money market account. At least that's where he told me the funds would be heading when all was said and done. The lot itself resembled a wax museum, or an embalming node, for cars inanimate, sure, clean as hell, but no seeming changes in the mix since that first time I came across the place. He said business was dead and on account of this transaction in transit, this was it, he was ready to cave, and this was all he needed me for. Fuck it, just for my own raw hide and its future health, karma and all, I consented to being the bodyguard. But no, I corrected myself, I'd be the guy doing all the talking and he would sit with his mouth shut in the passenger seat, and our agreement would transpire never again. He had nothing to lose, but Moser had scared him. He still had eyes snooping in on him at his place of residence, so he reported while I was back east, and he wasn't relaxed, not going even to the grocery store or a gas station. What a mess.

I wanted to be rid of this job, this guy, and the anguish I considered myself partly responsible for upon undertaking the case in the first place. I wasn't looking forward to the Rex affair, the Vitti ride, but the one saving grace still smoking at the end of my mind's gun was the possibility of transcendental reassessments at the shindig scheduled in two days' time at Cheesequarters. The Peyote Pussy. Some white unicorn of a concept that I never imagined could come into full frontal view at any time in an adobe, maybe stucco, compound dedicated to the advancement of pornographic film and all that comes along with it, be it rappers, accessories, and camaraderie via hallucination.

I was feeling friendly and asked Hel if he wanted to get a bite to eat or some coffee. He didn't want to be out in public, just to go home and wait until we were out for the delivery. He had two days, because tomorrow was out of the question. I instructed him to arrange the meeting, the drop off, the delivery, two days' time, high noon. And I left.

At the diner, Satch's, Dohltrey showed up and didn't make any attempt to act like we were just running into each other.

"How's Bobby?" I spewed.

"What are you saying?"

"You know who. You know where."

"I know where. Not who. We're all independent operators. There's no branches connecting the roots."—I kind of understood him, envisioning a vertically integrated bureaucratic regime with no connections on the bottom—the field ops, the roots so he said—so only the canopy types had the information to assign orders. He continued, "Now, that you're home, home base more accurate, it's best you stay put."

"You get a bonus or something if I do?"

"Well, if you don't, I probably make out better because I can get more funds to do more reco, but then again, that's just a pain in the ass."

"I hear ya."

"Not loud or clear enough. You've been a raging cough I can't seem to cure, and I'm tired, and now that summer's ending, I need a vacation."

"You shoulda come to New York."

"Are you crazy? What kind of vacation is that?"

"Ha, I see what you're saying, but keep an open mind."

"It's not like I ain't been there. My mind was open. Now, it's fried."

"You can't blame it on the place."

"I'm not here to argue. I'm here to get your signature, so we're not liable."

"Liable for what?"

"I'm just kidding. There are no papers or anything. Just handle your last loose end, privy to Lambert, and you can get back to whatever it is you do."

"What if I don't feel like getting back to whatever it is . . . I do?"

"By then, it won't matter."—We drank our coffee for a while and the waitress smiled at us both when she refilled our mugs. We smiled back. He broke the silence. "I gotta say, screw your racket. There's some sort of envy that's built up in me the past week or so, since you've been gone."

"I tend to charm even those I don't mean to."

"Bite me, Jeanny. Your snake charming doesn't deserve any recognition."

"Hey, when I take a look down there, I'm blind to all else."

"Figures."

"Can it all be so simple?"

"In a way, it's just that going over the numbers, you're gonna make out pretty good when this comes to a close. Hell, not quite like Brubaker, but enough to rode off over the horizon without a worry, at least for a while."

"Well, it's not like you don't have the means to do so. Just the balls, maybe, are lacking."

"If you knew what I knew, you wouldn't try a thing."

"I'm glad I don't."

"Stay glad."—He paid for my coffee, I don't know why, and left. That seemed pointless, as far as an angle, but maybe he wanted to see me off one last time before we both vanished beyond the point of crossing paths ever again. A feeling of mutual respect was rare these days, and though he'd never admit it, it was there.

I pulled out a card from Dynamo buried in a fold in my wallet and inspected it like the astronauts in Kubrick's space odyssey at the monolith. Now that I think of it, it must have looked more like the primates touching and feeling and cowering in its presence the way I looked then. No matter, there was nothing more to uncover. It was all bare bones, naked on the surface, and breaking it down into atomic components of logic and reason and explication was impossible to contemplate, conceptualize, or theorize, without sounding insane—or better yet, not. I tore it in two and put it in the empty coffee mug and went on my way. The sunset was pink like salmon and since it was already over the Santa Monica Mountains' ridges, I could rise inside that fine sight, avoiding brake lights and blinded drivers.

I drank a bottle of wine to go to sleep and got caught up looking at the veins in my toes and upwards into my foot pads and ankles. I took a mental note to focus in on these organic components once I got under the peyote veil. But before the wine was half done, I checked the movie times for the Perrault and thought I'd be late for the first ten minutes; *Burning Rubber* was at a venue I could make it to. I went. I enjoyed it, for its simplicity and well-executed action sequences. The montage of guns, girls, and steel was numbing, exactly what I needed. And the way it ended was a tragic play on comedic whims, kind of like *The Bicycle Thief,* that Italian flick where in spite of it all, things don't settle the way you expect in Hollywoodland's petrified forest of hardship and adversity defeated. Some high school kids were pissed upon exiting the theater, but a sequel of revenge was still on their want-to-see lists on account of the after credits teaser. All in all, there were worse ways to spend thirteen bucks.

13

I SHOULD have passed on the second half of that bottle of cabernet sauvignon. During the onslaught of traffic laborers in the morning, I guess it was those eggs I made myself queasing up my system that forced me to make a pit stop at a rank establishment on Ocean Avenue to dispel the wind. Then, I was tardy to the affair with Rex—He was not too pissed, emphasis on too, but the coffee only massaged my bowels into greater disarray. Other than that, I thought I had cleaned up the cake for the secretary's birthday rather handsomely and signed the agreements with competence and gusto. I didn't bother to read the fine print, but I probably should have.

Out the window of the bungalow office set up on the lot, I got caught up in the sights of myriad workers dodging about, to and from sound stages, prop houses, wardrobe closets, and the occasional savvy player in a convertible braking to a stop for a chat that could lead to an actress dame popping into the car for a ride or delaying the inevitable, for now. Huddled voices in cliquey circles equipped with clipboards and wireless hearing communicative devices, and dudes with baseball caps and sunglasses or hiking boots getting harangued by guys with long curly hair and band concert T-shirts. Hell, the studio on a day-to-day had enough stories to go around a few times. The meta movie of the machine, personified via Hollywood and all that that entails. By and large, I coasted through the meeting, shook some hands, held some farts and some straight faces, laughed a few times, and took on a victory cigar for good blessings going forth. The exact title they designated to me was Creative Consultant, and they made it up to me how far involved I would go, no reservations.

I set up an appointment for lunch with the producers, besides Rex, and one with the screenwriter Ollie Breeze. Had to be a pseudonym, but Ollie was an enjoyable name to enunciate. He implied he wanted me over his right shoulder during the course of development but worried about the lack of closure in the tentative third act so discussions followed. We needed more character arcs and value systems imbued in their realism, was what he claimed he wanted to accomplish. No matter that I couldn't agree less, for the life of me, it was a better bet in my gut to just be cool, be mutual, and get down to the actual process and maybe something would come of it. Stick to the sights for meta interpretation, not the words. I kept this to myself, naturally.

Rex requested I accompany him to another Cabot House fling with two new editorial leeches, but I declined, fortunate commitments to an airport ride.

The airport was a nightmare. I picked out a spot on the backend of the loop where arrivals came and opened the trunk and stood outside on the walkway to have a smoke. I riddled my frustration at being on the bottom level, hence the arrivals level, by brooding on the metastasis of the Hollywood deus ex machina witnessed earlier. Hell, some camera man, security, could rehash all the footage into a movie of the moviemaking process and pit the operatives around the arena into a cause and effect sequential farce, hell, even a splice of life. At the very least, a documentary. Or to the devil's chagrin, a reality show centered on the underpinning man to man processes and results, the aftermaths of studio broilings and brawn and burn. The traffic cop nodded me to move the ride, and I nodded at the cigarette, and he walked the other way.

Vittoria texted me she had landed, but the flight was held up in the traffic on the edges of the landing strips, and until the gate opened, she'd be stuck in place. What a fiasco.

The studio big wigs had granted me a retainer and weekly salary of quite high marks for creative consultation, aka, a title they just give you but do not remember to define, and I thought of going to the flux capacitor bar at the edge of the airport to wait but stopped because by the time I'd move my car, move my body, get a drink, come back down, and go to help her with luggage, or even if I didn't, the time would be a wash absent of any leisure or relaxation. Guess it had to be my fault for not expecting delays that should just be considered inevitable, and so I got in my car and looped around the roads bordering the doors to doors to gates to air until my phone alerted me that the time was right. I wish I could say that after departing the studio and having one of those rare windows where the seas part in the ocean of grind-it-out Angeleno traffic, I pulled up to the baggage claim, and she walked outside, and it was a moment of serendipitous clarity that I could remember for the rest of my life yet to be lived. But it wasn't. When I did pull up, I was parked left of her down the way behind a couple of town cars and taxis and one old Ford, and she looked to and fro and couldn't spot me; she looked cute in her own sort of innocent, longing way. Credit the micro cosmos of clearing the path ahead on the parked rightmost lane because it opened up, and I was able to lurch the car, roly-poly style up to the door she came out of and still stood suspended in front of. The smile on her face was as good as it could have been, and I didn't need any more to take down my personal offenses. Sure, she only had two small bags that I ended up hauling up to the trunk, but I missed the fantasy turned real of smooching on the causeway in a unity of spirits and bodies that I could crave only with a worthy one like her before me. But that wasn't really going through my mind, not at least 'til I saw two different couples do the dream and make it real as we pulled out. Or I could just do the same at a train station, but it wouldn't be so epic. Fuck it.

She didn't expect me to take her all the way to Carpinteria just yet, if ever, but she surely wanted me to, eventually. I considered an invitation to the Peyote Party but decided against bringing it up because it was better not to, then—she would pass and not care. Instead, I avoided the details and revealed I had prior engagements for the night to come, and she didn't ask what specific engagements they were, stayed silent in thought for thirty seconds, and then asked if I could break them. *"Something on your mind?"* I wondered.

"I can bring out the big guns and say there's some party in the hills by the county line and you'd probably comply, maybe, but the truth is, I don't intend on going to any kind of thing that social, so no."

She wasn't going to admit anything, and why should I? It wasn't my place, and the time was long gone. Maybe that is the crux of the matter that the east really told me out loud, bold, unforgiving. An old folk rock song from when rock wasn't a gimmick came on the tuner. It was called, "Blue Tangles," and I remembered it being one of the ones we had danced to at an isolated nook over the Pacific a long time ago. Her silence didn't give away any remainders of a memory, so I asked if she wanted a cigarette, she said no, in a nod, and looked away to the sights out of the passenger window, leaning against her scuffled up scarf as a pillow. I take it she didn't remember, better yet, didn't want to, and my romantic recall made me fell like a weak, no good slicker.

By the end of the cigarette, the song had changed to a headbanger anthem from the hair era and that feeling had lapsed. Thank the devil. When we got to the 405, I kept going straight and she looked over, and

I said, "Isn't it the first week of every month that they got the flea market over the way?" She smiled and that was enough. Logic: shopping cures. I knew ahead of time I would just lose my place in the junk area with blow up dolls, fountains, cupid statues, and the occasional record bin while she numbed herself with grassroots consumption, and she'd come find me with a gem I expected and all would be restored. Guess I'm a simpleton. It's okay—the way it is.

When she found me, she smiled and tapped me on the shoulder to get my attention, and she had in her other hand one of those snow globes that if you shake it, they typically get a flurry of snowflakes. Only this one was a beachfront with stucco houses and when she shook it, the waves careened up and down and a surfer bobbed his way before settling down. A tourist trinket that could go in a box in a closet but a worthwhile one for the separation and a pick me up for being stuck with each other for a little while longer with no chance we'd give in to carnal cannibalism and eat each other away at the insides. I knew I needed a drink. The traffic settled before school dismissal and after worker bees had their lunch breaks expire, so I got that drink fast, at Randolph's, and she ate a late afternoon omelette. With a spruce of energy, she was back on her feet, jiggling her left one, so I knew she was excited and full of zesty fire, and I only added to her pleasure. She encouraged me to actually make an effort to contribute for the Rex production and that it could lead to greener pastures and opportunities with the snap of a finger. "You'd be surprised, really," she reiterated.

I believed her but didn't want to sound like a sucker and said, "I'm not too worried. Not at all."—She let me keep going because that wasn't something she would grant a response to, the apathy. "But, I tell you, I like being off the grid."

She said, "Don't kid yourself. The time where that was a thing, especially in America, is passed."

"Not in my head, and that's all that matters."

"I'll give you that, babe, but you know, I'm just hoping you keep an open mind and take it for what it is worth, what it could be worth, you know, it could be something you never imagined or expected."

"I don't deny what you're saying. I just don't need to put myself in a position where I get played the wrong way."

"Don't kid yourself, again. Your temper's cooled, from what I've seen. Doubt any pencil pusher will make it come afire again."

"It's not that. I just feel like when I'm there, I'm really not. Like it is not happening around me, and I need a drink."

"That's almost a terrible way to put it, but there could be worse."

"If I have to do something I don't want to do, best make it on my terms."

"Well, when all of us are jet-setting sleuths with hands in everyone's pockets, I guess I'll come back and talk to you."

She nodded her chin to her left shoulder and grinned. I maintained my facial expression for a couple of seconds, didn't blink, took a loud breath, and drank my drink. In a word, yeah.

I started up again. "You're close enough."

I took her up Highway 1 to Topanga Canyon to drop her off at her girl's retreat compound. I was set to give her a ride the day after the Peyote parlor and planned to crash at her sister's up north to conclude that business.

14

THE SUN looked like an egg over easy, disintegrating into the plates we call clouds as we pulled up to the gate of Open Door. At the start, I took a cab to the lot, met Hel, got in the Jag, went. He was fidgety, looked like he didn't sleep much, purple-red under-eye bags, a scent of trashy body odor, and lots of scratches to the nine o'clock shadow on his neck. He looked like shit and he told me he felt like it, too. All bent up. I gave him my special formula, an antidote via electronic pen, vapor nicotine, plus a concentrated bud wax. He kept quiet for a while, guess it was the light and the mood it brought of seeing out far ahead, like the future was capable of accurately predicting, at least that's how I maneuvered the highway to the Valley veering from the fast lane over four lanes to transfer to the 101. The junction still smelt of sewage. I had learned to ignore that sign. So be it.

He kept urging me to go over the plan when we got off at exit 29 Valley Circle slash Mulholland Drive, and as we went north on the Valley Circle, he demanded a pick me up, to take the edge off his high strung paranoia and angst. Being a skipper of the ship for a lousy crew is one thing, but when there is no crew and there are just passengers, in particular one no gut, low down dummy, it gets annoying. A hassle impeding the serene drive to the distance ahead absent of brand names, pedestrians, and traffic lights. He got a red bull caffeine drink instead of coffee at the last gas station before the canyon dictated the change in time-space. This was when the sun dried out over the reservation land, the conservatory of nature, and the gate with the first logo that meant anything, read OPEN DOOR. The O and D were overlapping one another and though they may have been dyed blue, the paint was seeping together into some sort of hole. Guess Dynamo wasn't out of my system just yet, and heck, this was unfamiliar, but I could bet things wouldn't pan out in such an unexpected way that danger could really take hold. But for Hel, once passed the gate, he felt it crawl up his spine like the cool metal of the chamber of a gun, so he said, and I laughed, thinking of the chill of an ice cube a girl surprises you with to keep you on your toes. I told him not to worry and to have one of my smokes. The sentiment should imply relaxation and thus safety, indirectly, so I hoped. Thank everything and everyone the ride was over because he kept fiddling with the radio, too, and to the point where I had shut it off to avoid the lack of taste.

The road was paved and sparsely lit by artificial means, but the sun shone the right amount in its descent to coat the sights with a blanket of dilapidated melting ketchup, maybe diluted with mustard or Saucy Susan—a tan apricot color. Around a ravine, we hit the flatland, and it was sure was vast. Sprawled out in multiple viewing planes with runways and vast hangars that looked from afar like giant ice coolers crossed with typewriter cases, on account of the roofs and the way they curved. With the windows slightly open, it was awfully silent, but it was peaceful not holding suspense or tension. Okay, maybe it was holding tension for passenger Dante, but he had no more excuses. I was done with him, momentarily.

Just when we got to the vast expanse of flat, the guy at the second gate pointed us northeast to where the spotlights were coming on. There, we'd find Moser. He was taller than I expected, around 6'3" or 6'4". And that tattoos seemed suffocated by his sleeves and collar.

He had those junkie eyes, that Hel had emphasized, those ones like a bull befuddled in a post-heat frenzy that never stopped simmering but didn't quite boil over. Carried himself like he was intimidating: chin up, shoulders way back, eyes without blinks but not intense. He stared me down hard, but I stayed in the car and let Hel go and delegate. Bad call. Moser lit up a smoke and stared death down through the windshield, so I got out. I said Hel didn't feel quite secure, so I was going to come along for comfort. Moser smirked and shrugged but didn't seem to care. But he looked back at Hel to his left, and if Hel had had a place to crawl back into and hide, he would have most wanted to then. "That wasn't the agreement."

He slapped Hel on the side onto one knee. It looked like an overreaction on Hel's part but then again, it was not expected and Moser was not a boy. I butted in—"What's the trouble?"

He waited a couple of seconds before looking up at me from Hel, "You know . . . you."—On the second *you*, his eyes bulged like those of a blowfish. But immediately, he had the capriciousness to laugh and change the mood, the atmosphere, and as the sun came to a vanishing point over the mountains, the smoke bellowed out of his black hole between jagged teeth and the lights were on behind him. Devilish but cool.

"Didn't realize the car trade was so criminal."

"When you deal with scum like this," at Hel, "there's no reason not to make it feel like it is."

I tossed him the keys—He waved a flare just to be dramatic, and some guy brought the Cabriolet up beside him. The guy looked Hispanic or foreign from the desert in the light, caught a gaze of 'stache and goatee—He handed over the keys to Moser, and Moser threw them over to me. I caught 'em. Hel looked like he was breaking down.

Moser glanced down at him again, then at me. "Oh, look what I've done." He helped Hel up, patted him on the back, and popped the Cabriolet trunk open. Hel went over, and I couldn't see the whole of him or what he was looking at. Moser didn't watch what he was doing, like he had nothing to worry about, Hel was no threat, and so he came over and wrapped his arm around me real close and turned so we were both facing west, backs to Hel, and we started walking. I didn't like how he was so close. Before he could finish, "I just want you to know," we had been slide tackled to the pavement, and Hel had grabbed the keys from the pavement and scrammed to the car that chirped when he clicked the remote. The one that responded was the Jaguar.

He started to flee. What an idiot. Moser put his hands on the hood of the Jag and stared maliciously at Hel behind the wheel, snarling haphazard frustration. Moser got out of the way and was patient for the pursuit. He signaled to me with a hand, and we got in the Cabriolet. He wanted to drive, and I thought that made sense, since it was his car at stake. I wondered what was in the trunk. That thought died fast as we picked up speed and flew blindly into the dark. The headlights couldn't do too much after we left the range of the spotlights, especially when Hel turned off his high beams and went stealth, and then so did Moser. The seat was too tight for him so he looked like a rabid clown gone amok from a circus, sleeves rolled up and the colors only added to the comparison. He punctured the gearbox with relentless heaves and spotted Hel making his way behind us, the way snakes in paintball get behind the team on the offensive. The e-brake couldn't handle the momentum, and we spun out to lose ground. With the parking lights, we tried to find some skid marks left by the Jag but it was hard to tell whose were whose, especially in the aftermath of the spinout. Moser kept slamming his hands on the wheel like he was all done feeling wronged. When we got to the far most hangar farther east, a plane landed not a hundred feet away. It was weird because there were no guide lights on any runway. The plane cannoned into the side view mirrors and stayed there. Moser got out and motioned me to, conceding defeat. Fuck it, Hel didn't take what was his. He'd be dealt with later, so I assumed. But I was played.

When the hangar doors opened, the Jag was in plain sight, alit in the smooth cement tracking ground that looked like concrete ice against the pellucid overheads. There was no plane in the hangar, just large boxes blocking the view of the other half of the hangar. The hangar gates already began to shut when we stepped in, and I figured there was nowhere to go anyhow, abandoned on a manmade desert, so I waited for what I had got myself ridden into to play out.

Moser had gone out of sight, and when I stood my ground, the lights went dim and then down, and the jab to the back of the head had to be coming soon, and it did, and I went into the black. It didn't fully knock me out but it belted my senses enough so two guys had to grab me by my armpits and drag my feet against the concrete as they took me around the boxes to the other half of the hangar. I lifted my head up and one of the guys said, "Cabron!" and when they sat me on a chair, it was like an interrogation set-up in an old movie, with all the lights out except for one on the table. On the other side, Moser gaily took a seat, and my head was still down so he pushed it up from the chin. He leaned his head down and eyes almost rolled up, checking if I was back to earth. I wasn't entirely, but he started anyway. He laughed for an extended charade, the joke on me, obviously. I looked up at him, devoid of all expression, only fatigue on my face and took a cigarette out of my chest pocket. He lit it, and then I felt my head. There was a fat bump, but it'd heal. Hel came up beside Moser, then by me, and said, "Oh, ugh, oh, oh, dear, ugh, Jean." And I shoved him away without looking, but he didn't bear the blunt of the shove well. I think he said sorry again, but I wasn't paying attention.

"What happened to Hel?"

"Hel's gone. Trunk, suitcase, money, freedom."

"Maybe that explains the plane."

"What do you care, now? You've done your part. Now—"

"Wait . . . you're telling me he got his because you got yours . . . mine."

"Bingo."

Sighed, but not out of lament or melancholy, just a lack for words at the ludicrous turn of the conversation. "You could have just asked."

"No, we wanted Hel to feel like he had a job to do, a responsibility, be on the same team. Something called loyalty."

"What happened to just good guys versus bad guys?"

"Watch your mouth. You don't want me to mistake you for a sucker."

"Well, you're not beating me to a broken record, so it can't all be that big a deal."

"Yes and no. But by God, you look vulnerable."

"Eat a peach."—I was waiting for it; not the punch, but the threat of one—And fortunately according to the pain principle, I guess, Moser didn't threaten me. To be honest, I wish he had slugged me because I could've had the last laugh, make him seem stupid. But, he strained. And I didn't have to wait for who had to be pulling the strings to make an encore bow.

15

CHARLIE HAD a gun. It was just for show. I almost laughed but made it out to be a cough. I wasn't worried. Maybe I should have been. Actually, I guess I should have been, but even my arrogance doesn't concede to defeat at the sight of a deadly weapon. It looked natural for him, like he was some new person I didn't know, only had heart bits and pieces of rumors through gossip vines and trails of print and screen. He didn't sit down but he circled me and caressed the skin on my neck with the cool metal of the Ruger; it felt violating, like I was a dog getting pet in such a way to make me feel like I was just that, a dog at the behest of some master.

"I apologize for it having to be this way. It should work out fine, so you don't worry."

"Why'd you go and admit that to me, Charlie?"

I never saw him again. He did not say a thing. Nothing. Gone but for the moment before, in retrospect, a specter of haunting idiosyncrasies and representations thereof. I was stumped. It was silent for a while and with Moser still there, I thought it best to follow his lead, keep quiet for a while and wait for him to make an illusive move. It was clear he had no more power than I, in this case, none, and that to the powers that be had already dictated how the situation was going to unfold. A siren went off, for three beeps, not quite like an alarm clock or an emergency alert, but as a signifier of some course of action. The course of action was the transference of documents by Moser to me, placed on the table in front, and for me to take in their black and white images as objective truth, and for me to accept them at face value.

What they were worth was invaluable. It showcased my bank account, a statement of the past month's deposits and withdrawals, transfers, and trades. Very personal stuff, my life's receipts, permanently marked and affront to a private citizen. Sure, it showcased my lack of disciplinary spending habits, but the chord meant to strike hard home were the payments made from Dohltrey via Dohltrey and Company LLP. What that was I was never made aware of but upon the further analysis, with some page flips of my portfolio, it became loud and clear. See it as payments, sure the one by Brubaker for Vittoria and her play-acted disappearance, followed by the three lump sums granted via Dohltrey for services rendered to Dynamo, even though I didn't sign anything, they were marked. The check copies were legitimate, in that they could be held up as truthfully authentic and genuine from a court's perspective, and that my fees had been timed to be infused to my account at the most dubious of coinciding outside events.

Like Dohltrey had said, I was to make out of this scenario with flying colors, specifically green or gold, and with my newly minted wealth mine and mine alone, there had to be consequences, and I was not thinking about taxes. They didn't need to spell it out for me and then, I was glad Charlie hadn't said a thing in the first place. The first payment was not processed until the date of the IPO. The second, the last weekday, Friday, the week of the New York trip and the crime. And the third, the day after the scandal and subsequent rise in share price. Based on possible allegations and circumspect elucidations, it was plausible to concede I was an insider. At least the paranoia could tell me this much. What really struck low notes and gave me hives were the investment moves: the trades ordered executed to time with the activities of the company since public options were granted. Caught red handed was an archaic, ironic way to put it. Because the numbers shown black, but what the black represented was green, and a heck of a lot of it. After I had let the information simmer into my being, I took a look up and by that time, all visible life forms had disappeared, were invisible, gone.

I was alone and free to go. Both cars were still there with the keys still inside them both, but the plane had taken off and was gone gone. I didn't want to take the time to wait for proper transportation, a cab on the concrete desert, so I took the Cabriolet, only to the end of the property, disposed of the keys into the darkness of the backseat for I don't know why, I wasn't thinking, and walked the rest of the way out of the ravine and through the canyon to Valley Circle Road. It was an off-shade of black close to a hint of navy on account of the lunar light awfully resembling the moon the night I had spent on the reservation. When I got to the main road, my phone service showed positive with a couple bars ascending, and I called for a cab to pick me up at the mouth of the canyon, a few miles up, no, south, where Roscoe Boulevard ended. I told the cab to wait, if I was not there at the proper time, give or take a couple minutes, but the driver was not mad at me for making him wait. So it wasn't rude. Anyway, straight to the Peyote Party; I needed to get away from myself.

I didn't consider myself the loser of the scenario. Heck, according to verifiable records, that money was mine, and in the world I grew up in, with love and honor and the like absent from the scenario, green tended to be the sole purveyor of victory. Of course, it felt like a staged one. Not a pity victory but a victory of nothing. As if the pile of chips were made out of sand disintegrating through my fingertips. But freedom has its ways. I had just experienced a merciful God's grace, benevolence of a nebulous entity of commerce. Heck, I couldn't complain. I hadn't had to bring a gun, my streak was at an all time high since the last time I had thought I may need one for safety and security, and on top of that, the client of my concern had been handsomely compensated out of his seeming inevitable demise turned victory. Heck, Hel must have been on a plane to paradise, flying private, beyond the confines of first class, with a luggage of loot, and a plethora of future pleasure guaranteed by said loot. It was all right for me to serve the purpose of the sacrificial lamb, martyred to blackmail, sabotaged to suspension, but as long as the blackmail was kept in the dark, the suspension never turned to confinement, and I could still dictate where I went on the territorial expanse, I was okay. I was alive and free enough. I wasn't even mad at him. Just as his responsibilities in the form of all material possessions as in the lot had disintegrated into a smothering mother's hands to be dealt with to some other end, so was my present workload, the curtain holding all the glasses and figurines in place on the table to come to an implosion of some sort, had been thrust out from under them so they had nowhere to go. The map was gone. Or had everything just melted into some amorphous form, magma at the core of a deep shaft that was yet to cool off into a form of considerable consequence?

The cabbie turned on the radio, and I snapped out of my ritual analysis. It wasn't even a good song; it sounded like some clone of Madonna that had missed the correct intermingling of DNA or some chromosomes were not duplicated properly, but the sexual innuendos and the beat could have been good if they had never been wed together on that particular song. I think it was called "Joker Face," or something, but the point being, that I was on to the future. I asked the guy to switch to another station, he asked what kind of music, and I said, "Anything as long as it's tasteful." He put on some tribal instrumentals that may have reflected his background. I thought the melodies and droning noises set me right to prepare for the metamorphosis ahead into the starless night.

16

T HE PARTY had shifted locations, and I had forgotten about this detail until we got to the first one. It was at the house I'd been used to going to, and where I had dropped off the honorable goods themselves. It looked back to normal, only a SUV in the driveway and sports playing on the television visible through the front lawn. No bodily motion. I kicked my feet in the grass and waved down the cabbie before he had a chance to say no because he was bound to another stranded wanderer somewhere nearby. The stars that were so visible up above at the concrete desert had shifted to ground level, slightly above at the traffic signals. It was okay, I didn't think it'd be much good for me to get into my head any grand ideas about illusion and the profundity of the cosmos so it was good that I was out of sight of the stars, blind.

There was no traffic in the Valley on the streets he took, avoiding Reseda or another throughway, instead taking Wilbur south, a residential street so we could party in peace. I didn't mind that the meter cost me more. The come up was key, and prior to the come up, the preparation. I was getting into the zone, so I kept telling myself.

When we hit Ventura Boulevard, I stopped thinking.

The house was on a dead end, somewhere up the hills, but I didn't need to bother to check specifics, the cabbie had digital navigation. He bid me farewell, and I had to navigate through myriad cars parked representing all sorts of paths that had come to a stop at the site: limos, pickups, smart little Euro cars, some lifesize Hot Wheels types, and a leitmotif of German luxury. All in all, no one that got there early was getting out anytime soon. They were parked for a long haul to the sun's reappearance, at minimum. This had to have been an enormous monstrosity because I noticed the walls to neighboring fortresses made the houses themselves absent to the naked eye, not due to the darkness but due to the lights that led into the wide open expanse. The landscapes were still in development, lots of dirt still, but the house itself was of a royal nature, an ode to the ranches only existent through black and white photos from the time before freeways altered the Valley into the infernal luminosity.

The front doors were open. There was no courtyard, but there was a powder room beneath the first staircase on the left, and I did my best to clean off the blood from my face. I did a fine job and was lucky there was no obnoxious swelling. I infused my mouth with green mouthwash, splashed a lot of water on my face, and spritzed whatever cologne was in the drawer to mitigate the risk of stinking up my immediate surroundings once the drugs would take hold. Nothing like proper hygiene prior to a hallucination. Comfort is key.

Meandering through the house, I came to see there was no sign of camera or production equipment, and it hit me. Maybe he had just taken up the place to rent for his own residential use. What a slick player. Cheese found me in a drawing room and was shirtless, hair flailing close to his mid back section, backwards cap on, all black, and a couple wrist chains complemented his 100 cigarettes that had to be menthol. It was confirmed it was menthol when he jumped on my back and put the cigarette in my mouth, so I was piggybacking him around. He looked like a kid high on drugs, to put it plainly. Cheese driving without the car, I absorbed into the assimilated fray of goers and comers conned to think they had won, the war was over, America was in power for perpetuity, and all was glorious in the confines of the structure we had found ourselves in. And the best part was that it was casual. I refrained from any liquor prior to the intake of the drugs, but partook in some collaborative joint and blunt rolling and subsequent smoking on some finely placed couches. There was boxing on the two television screens, and though we were not heavily invested in the fights, it was still a weekday and it was not Pay-Per-View; the televised spectacle further fueled the ruckus. After an hour, Cheese winked at me and I saw him, a couple guys he worked with, and some cute Red Riding Hood types go into exit mode, and I followed to the guest house past the pool and up some stairs through some foliage to begin the process.

The guesthouse was bigger than an average American green lawn, white fenced, nestled away on some dilapidated drug masonry estate. We were safe, the walls were too far away to realize that we were not the only people that existed in the fiefdom, and the processions were marked by the silence from the party below because we were so far up and beyond their reach. It felt positive. And I quickly lost any sense of self for a momentary lapse of reason metamorphosed into an involute state of succumbing to the hallucinogenic powers that loosened all notions of physical and limited sensation. I was lost in a state where being found was not the point but the thing to be prevented and avoided at any notion.

Tracking time was lost but if I had to guess back, it was somewhere between two and four hours when the girls began to take off their clothes. I'm pretty sure most of them were not under the influence of the peyote because I had not seen them partake and to add to that, they moved way too lithely to have been undergoing any mystical transfiguration of spirit. If only I had had a tangible artificial mask like the one worn by the Phantom of the Opera, I could have convinced myself this was a masquerade at the Roman Forums.

My reference was close enough in practice because my spirit was sound, and I was led off by two nudes, one black haired, one blonde, to somewhere I didn't know how to get to and the orgy proceeded like a personal vendetta. I was the blunt of their sexual vengeance on allegorical levels, the one cock to be pained and pleasured by more holes than I could fill at once. I was enthralled. Throbbing, not groaning, and I was an everyday multiple, a groaner and pusher. I left the moans to them, the throbs from my heart palpitated like it was getting vacuumed through my chest cavity into their heaving lungs and supple breasts. I lost track of who was who in the minimal light, and I thought it was Harley's face on one of them and Vittoria's face on the other. And then they shifted bodies and the interchange commenced for a few minutes before it began to distract from my pleasure, and so I closed my eyes and they did not return. Eventually, the candles burnt out and in the dark, the familiar faces were not capable of haunting me because there was no desire left.

So after I came on their breasts or bodies—one of their breasts definitely, but I think I may have missed the mark on the other one—we laid naked and smoked cigarettes. I stared at my ember, didn't pay attention to either of them, and in the ashing ember before it turned to stone-Medusa-ash that would fall, it stayed in place and I saw an angelic Cupid morph and turn its head before swallowing up into an amalgam of orifices all the same color. I stared at a microscopic level, the darkness of the room only hyper realizing the observatory power of vision held in my left hand. I chainsmoked another and let Cupid travel from one to the next, and he reappeared on the second cigarette, this time he looked older, and more like a teenager, and he was smothered by pure fire. No metaphors or transcendental visions. Then, we resumed fucking.

Fucking is the wrong word though. It felt more ritualistic and whimsical like this had some purpose and it was greater than the sum of its parts. But for my part, it felt like all I could ever ask for and need. It's not like any notion of time passing matters at any remote level under the influence of a conscious mind-bending drug. After we got sweaty for a while they fell asleep, and since I had unplugged the clock and my watch was in a coat pocket, the high didn't seem to be slipping away. Sure, I felt more alert, from the rush of the orgasm, but after the orgy, I hoped someone else could be up and ready to smoke until the more intense high led to the more subdued one, the hallucination standard, the peyote was already added to the marijuana, and then to sweet, sweet sleep.

I got my wish. When I awoke at sunlight, the girls and I had a normal round. We were cordial and exchanged contact information. Then, I left.

17

I HAILED a ride with some randoms leaving at the same time. They took me down to the main boulevard, and I had them drop me at a diner so I could refuel while waiting for the cab. I stunk of sex and aching muscles. Overall, the daylight was still summer seeming even though it was already tagged for the end of September. I didn't keep keen track but the number on my watch said one, and I tended to trust it to its function. The cab came and got me, and I fell asleep on the way back to my place over through the Sepulveda Pass. My phone had been dead, and I let it charge while I showered, and my phone happened to ignite onward, there were two voice messages. The first was from Harley, and I didn't feel like hearing what she had to say so I skipped it and listened to the second from Vittoria who asked if I was still willing and able. I was and I texted her so. I popped a few Adderralls, extended release, to make sure my body didn't make me think otherwise, filled up the tank, and took Highway 1 up to Topanga to go and get her.

It was pretty normal.The ride got off to a positive start with the aesthetic appreciation for sailing up the sea of road beside the chops of the water and sand and wax-covered boards and bodies unrecognizable from a distance. It was good that I didn't have a convertible because if I did, she would have asked me to put the top down and the sun's rays would have baked me to a premature fatigue. We had the windows down and that was enough momentum in the quaint weather. There was not much traffic, just a couple other cars making the trip north when we passed El Matador State Beach and even less traffic when we passed the County Line. Neither of us talked, and I don't know if she wanted to or not. I was too busy keeping busy in my own vegetative post-traumatic mixed-drugs state. Not that that was a bad thing. Just a biological necessity.

She sparked a spliff and handed it off to me after a few pulls, and we shared it in silence, though the breezy air and howling organs of The Doors accompanied us. A gang of motorcycle riders passed us at this juncture and one of the bearded leathery fellas smiled as he passed her side. We followed them for ten miles or so because we had to stop off for drinks. Only waters and beers, just for the ride. We could have waited but both our mouths were parched from the lingering effects of the smoke. I took a look at her, too.

We avoided eye contact for the most part, comfortable just knowing we were next to each other and no drama could arise in the lack of words exchanged.

Amelie was not there when we arrived, and Vittoria said she had to rest and did just that. I stayed on the porch, and baked in the setting sun, and ended up listening to the voice message after Harley vibrated my pocket to question if I had listened to her message. She had said, something that did not matter, because I wasn't paying attention and after a minute or minute and a half of framing her lively mood on account of daily happenstance, she needed a favor but framed it as a pleasant request to meet, ride with me, and socialize in each other's company. I guess I was up to her standards rising on account of the Rex affair, maybe I was show-off worthy goods. I felt like shit though and did not have even dormant desire for more sex. Just booze. That was enough.

I took a nap on the couch just inside the porch, and when I woke up, it was an early dark, but I couldn't tell by just the lack of sun. Amelie was brewing some tea in the kettle, and Vittoria was still sleeping. When I came in, Amelie asked me what I had done. I gave her a look like, *What? Come again?* and waited for her to draw out her response to increase its impact. She was suave with it. the delay. "You'd have to have done some thing. When Vittoria doesn't talk much and gives me that look and just goes to sleep, it means something, especially with guys."

"Especially me."

"Not in particular . . . okay, especially you."

"It couldn't have been the drive."

"She's probably worried for a reason, if only you could tell me some thing, any thing at all."

"I did some peyote yesterday."

"Hell, you could have brought me up some."

"Ah, I should have. Next time."

"It can't have been as wondrous as the stuff the Chumash got on the reserve out here."

I smiled.

"—Do I look like I need worry about?"

"You always look like there's some dame worrying about you. As long as it's not me, fine. But if it's my sister, then I have to pick and pry and find out."

"Are you suggesting something?"

"Maybe you just cool it and relax, your face looks haggard."

"Thanks, I suppose I forgot my sunscreen."

"Or some self worth."

"Blows below the belt are allowed now, I see."

"Since when were they not?"

"I guess never."

"Okay, big shot. You're in my house. Just behave yourself and don't make her worry."

"And what if I can't control that?"

"You can't, but you're a man, just say you can do that for me."

"I can do that for you."

"Now I can make you a drink."

We went out on the porch and we shared a blanket and a joint.

"You better make your move."

"Whaddya mean?"

"Now or never."

"Just hand me that joint."

She did.

"—You know he asked her to marry him and all?"

"She told me, yeah."

"C'mon trooper, take a stand."

"It's not my place."

"No, it's my place, and I'm giving you free reign. Autonomy. Freedom."

"The choice has always been mine."

"That's where you're wrong, buster."

"How you say?"

"Fork it over."—I did. "All I mean is you were there first."

"Guess that counts for something."

"You bet, just give it a shot."

"What if I got my eye hogtailed for someone else?"

"Who ya kidding?"

I winked at her. She started giggling.

"You want me to take a ride with ya, Jean-O?"

I shrugged my shoulders but couldn't hit the smile.

"I won't admit defeat, but that doesn't mean I want to win."

"What a crock of shit."

"I thought that sounded like a reasonable excuse."

"It sure did."—She ashed it dead.

I got up to wash my face, but said, "Anyway, if you knew how deep this all went, you'd know that what you're suggesting for me to do would be suicidal. Lots of muddy consequences. Stress, struggle, the works."

"I'll stick with remembering the first excuse."

"Fair enough."—She muttered something under her breath when I went in, or maybe it was just a deep breath in and out because it was just not worth trying to communicate. I would not have gotten it, anyway. I left that night before Vittoria awoke. Maybe she already was, she just didn't want to come out of her room. I didn't want her to, either, and I'm glad she didn't. Emerging from the void of trips and visions, I always tended to reflect and reassess and try to see the world picture in a modified light, a healthier one, with some sort of gained wisdom that was sustainably healthy. In such a time like that one then, I made arrangements to come by and drop off some of the peyote, but Amelie wouldn't take it, said she could get it herself, but she said come by, on my own, if I wanted, and we could have some fun. I wasn't sure what she meant, but her pose hugging the doorpost looked mightily inviting, her scarf and hair twirling, and even some breast visible. I said, "What about her?" nodding my head toward the house, and she said, "She's gone." Pecked cheeks and got on my way.

When I got home, I called Harley. She said she'd pick me up and take me along to where she was going. She kept reiterating how she was so concerned that she could not reach me, that my phone had been dead, that I might have been lost lying dead or mucked up in some strange inaccessible place, mutilating myself to infamy. She was too melodramatic, but I appreciated the concern when she picked me up, got out of the car, and hugged me with luscious vigor. I told her to quit it after she was getting cumbersome, knees bent upward, and my neck and upper back weren't wanting to swing her around for more than ten seconds. I said, "Quit it or I'll start thinking you're my girl." She was offended and recoiled back into the driver's seat. "You coming, or what?"—I was.

I was still coming down to earth from the peyote, and when we crossed into the Valley down the 405, my stomach felt nauseated. I kept the feeling to myself and chainsmoked so it'd go away. Harley was driving like a maniac, swerving from fast lane to slow and back, like a snake on the hunt for some fleeing prey. It couldn't have helped my stomach, but I tolerated it. Where we were going anyway? She said, "Somewhere familiar—You'll be taken care of." Whatever the hell that meant, I was soon to find out.

She kept poking at me, touching me with her right arm, since I was on the passenger side, and kept saying things like, talk to me, I'm here for you, what's been going on, what's wrong, you've been acting funny lately. And I wouldn't have it. I wasn't hearing her for what she meant and just took it as irritating, annoying, stupid, and needy. She didn't cease her attack. I said, what, because I'm not doing a normal, banal workload, you get all upset that I may be spending my time doing other things. Who the hell was she to judge and determine what was best for me? Get the hell out.

Thinking it was endearing to swallow my pride for the sake of peace and quiet prior to judgment impairing copulations we were bound to be strung into later that night, I said I was cranky from the lack of rest I'd gotten as of late and that don't take this the wrong way but she was not the first pretty broad poking in on my emotional concerns that day. Not that there was anything emotional to be truly concerned about.

It turns out I was wrong in my assessment, for she went loose and head sprung into self-righteous bludgeoning. Here's some expert summation, "Are you serious? Lemme guess, your ex ex-girlfriend, another ride to Ventura, and another hope for no reason. You disgust me, sometimes, one of those times is definitely now."—Her high-pitched hisses coincided with some forceful wielding of the steering wheel and honks to accompany her reckless abandonment as she shifted between lanes. She slammed on the brakes way too fast for comfort upon exiting the freeway and let more spill. "Do you realize how pathetic this all looks?"—I almost said I did but kept my mouth shut. "Heck, I don't even know anymore. I hate seeing myself like this. Arguments are always better without mirrors around. But that's beside the point. Point being, get over her. Get over yourself. And get on with it. If you want to play out the tragic role, be my guest. I'm done." My blood pressure and heartbeat had been rising throughout the onslaught. Deep breaths, Jean, deep breaths, I kept telling myself. It only delayed the inevitable.

"Quit the melodrama, Jezebel."—She was appalled. But it did shut her up, and maybe if I had been cold and unforgiving from the start, all those fully disclosed sentiments could have been avoided. Maybe in another life. The way it was now, they were all out for me and her to see, in a pool of broken words and disagreeable feelings, stuck in the car now, and whenever we were done with what we were heading to, we'd still have to get by in each other's company. Perhaps it was the sick celibate underpinning of a platonic relationship, after the sexually deviant one had been curtailed, but we still thought each other considerably worthy of each other's attention, but that in that moment had been birthed to grow and fester. That's how I could reason it out, in some crackpot logic, because in cases like these, it would have been ideal to just have her stop the car, make it cinematic, have her get out, have me get out, and we'd have our backs turned to one another, and when one of us would turn around, probably me, I'd go up and pull her around like nothing else really mattered. That would have been cathartic and satisfying to all parties. But the way it was, that was not going to happen.

Seduction after a trip is circumspect, especially without a comparable dose of uppers to reignite dampened flames. Regardless, I made sure any attempt for my mind and body to harmonize in the inspiration of letting bygones be bygones and kisses be kisses to die a quick death. Stubborn pride was a better victor. At least its aesthetic surely was. I didn't bother to ask where we were headed, and by the time I recognized the entry to the southern hills past the main boulevard, I already figured right. We had returned to the hoax of a party, Cheesequarters migrated down and up into the Valley hills. Most of the cars looked the same, but I couldn't be sure because there was a clear path to the front door through the driveway, and Harley blocked that path with her car at its end. Judging by the sounds, it was more of the same with a jab of raucous banter and more obnoxious bass tones blaring through inefficiently soundproofed walls. How she connected through mutual accord was as good a mystery as any, and I was not really curious, just thought it was amusing how things to work like that, in concentric circles that occasionally merge and overlap and come together at times of inebriation and motion. When Harley took off her seatbelt, she turned to me, with a look of utmost desperation, like a little sister trying to tell her older brother to heed her words with dutiful care, "Just try to see it from where I am. You can't always be right."

"I can make it that way for me."

"But that's not the matter. Right, wrong, sort of, that's beside the point."—She got out of the car and started walking into the house.

I got out and said, "Then what do you mean?"

"Just hear me. Just listen, I'm not some authority figure. If those closest to you say the same things, in regards to you, your person, you should at least take what they have to say with some care. For us."

She carried on moving inside, and I stopped and smoked a cigarette and went around the back, letting her words go in one ear and out the other. But out the other was blocked up by the impeding bass, had to be hip hop, slow beats per minute, and my sights got caught up in naked women cavorting in the pool, alit and luscious. I saw Cheese in his natural state, shirtless in a jacuzzi with nudes in contact with all his arms and legs, and he quickly got out and still soaking, proceeded to talk to Harley. What the fuck was going on in this small world? Maybe I had introduced them but I guess either way, it made sense they could recognize one another from the connection to me. That was a simple way to put it. They spotted me and continued their conversation, perhaps plotting to reinforce the same thoughts through different voices to will me into submission.

I beelined to the bar and waited for an inevitable face to face confrontation. I considered submerging myself into witless social banter with the familiar cliques planted around the pool when I spotted a healthy target, a dame caught alone on a seat lounging and not caring, because she was not on some mobile device, or fiddling through her purse, but rather, just smoking a cigarette and sipping her cocktail with precision and relaxed motion. Fortune had me wrong because when I bound into action, Cheese interrupted my frame of sight. He said, "We should talk," and whisked me away inside the house. He said he was going to go to another party, to get away from the one that had not ceased for more than a few hours each morning when everybody slept dead since the last time I had been for the peyote, and that with the escape, I should accompany him. He noted his preference to Harley and suggested that she come along, or that a car would be picking us up. I said why bother with her, but he ignored or did not hear that and within ten minutes, we were out the doors, past the driveway, and in a town car, and they made me sit in the middle of the backseat, between them, with the excuse that if one of us was in the front, we'd be left out of the conversation. Stupid reason, especially because we didn't talk much. We were on the Westside eventually, somewhere between the 405 and the 101 where Hollywood starts and ends, and I was unsuccessful in determining where we were heading. We pulled up to Cedars Sinai and I gave them both a look of what's going on, and they said in unison, "It's best. Just do it for us." Myriad feelings veined through to my brain but more to my heart, and I lost control of myself. I grew livid, insulted, how could they, under my nose, through deceit and fraud ... without a single straight up sober confrontation beforehand ... at least in clear cut words. So we got out, and walked in to the emergency area, and saw a cracked out woman with someone's blood on her blouse, and it really mucked me up bad. Evil omen, dark.

Before we could get in the triage room, I realized I could still control what was going to happen to me, that it was not worth spiting my so-called friends by serving their desires and passing doctor-certified analysis to say I was able to be normal in normal condition, in normal freedom, and instead, decided to leave. The way I said it was, "One more cigarette before the overnight." They didn't really argue, especially after the sight of the deranged crackhead who had suffered in a way we didn't want to see any longer than we already had. So we went out for that cigarette, and the employee by the door motioned us away from it because of it being a hospital and all, and we complied.

When we were smoking, I gradually shifted toward the street and they caught on and were not going to stop my fleeing because they assumed I wouldn't do something that could look so foolish. I didn't. I definitely considered it, though. I didn't blink when I smoked, and I avoided eye contact with both of them. Harley was tearing up, I gathered, from the sounds of sniffles. It turns out that they had expected me to come, escorted me so when I went in, all I had to do was see an array of social workers and so did Cheese and Harley, at separate intervals. I explained my side of the story as they had been overtly concerned about my well-being, circumspect to drug use and an inability to keep track of my whereabouts and that it was all a big misunderstanding. I tried to hit on the first social worker and that did me no harm nor good. The second one, had an admirable rack bursting from her low cut top, and it distracted me up to the point where she conceded the best course of action could be the prescription of leveling drugs, limiting my maximum and minimum serotonin slash dopamine levels. This sounded terrible. And they tried to get me to go talk back with the original social worker I had been hitting on. I got kind of agitated when I realized Harley and Cheese had left the premises, at least that hospital floor, and had thus abandoned me to the system, for the system to sort out their problem about my person. I called for a cigarette, but they would not let me leave. It was quite an atrocious sight, a bunch of inexperienced sexually deprived young things determining what would be best for me, the rebel without cause, for they were there to see to my reprogramming to normalcy.

In ten minutes, after I had agreed to reconvene in the first chick's office and discuss my present position, there was an array of cops scattered in the waiting room upon my exit. And wow, I felt flattered but noticed their leader, an oaf of a fella named Grant, had his gun unholstered and his hand just itching to spring it free and ready for use, so I took a seat opposite him in the waiting room. The other cops were just as oafish, ogreish, brutish, chunky, and the two nearest to Grant and me had sunglasses and tribal and irezumi sleeve covering tattoos, and I thought they looked like characters in a children's comic fantasy tale. I kept my trap shut until spoken to but refused to break eye contact with Grant. He took a liking to this and asked what I wanted, said the cigarette, he cracked a smile, and we went down together. Me, in the centerfold with ten cops in the elevator, all squished in like bowling pins waiting to be struck. I struck the cop's match to my cigarette and the one named Lopez had one with me, too. We were at the back entrance now, on La Cienega, and there were lots of cop cars and one ambulance and all had their lights flashing, so people were gathering across the street to take in the pretty lights.

After the cigarettes came to an end, they measured my blood pressure and heartbeat in the ambulance, and I had a police escort to the next hospital ward where they'd chosen to put me. The hospital was Saint John's, and it was closer to the water so I got to take in that air before it'd be forbidden for some time yet to be determined. Maybe I still had a couple friends on the force because I felt lucky to be at a more low key establishment, by the water. It was a wholesome positive, as well.

I told the doctor my story. He was young, probably fresh out of medical school or still doing his residency, and he said, just sleep it off, take a drug test, and we'll take it from there. I was on a 72-hour period, I gathered, and in a couple days they'd have to make me sign a voluntary form to keep me imprisoned for "treatment" they called it. I slept it off the night pretty swell and was not bothered at all. When I woke up though, I still felt all bummed that the friends I had had treated me that way. Felt like I'd been subjugated to the bureaucratic system, and if I was raped, so be it. I was out of their sight and became a concern in only an abstract sense of the word. But, I didn't want to get ahead of myself, so I waited and bided my time as best as I could, avoiding the crazies, the suicidals, and the disgusting ones that shit themselves, so I could be on my own.

In a place like that, the worst thing one can do to his or her self is get used to the residents, because if you consider them normal, you might as well stay right in there with them. This scared me. It also scared me that there was no place to jack off, really, except the shower, which had poor water pressure, but the thought that my roommate and the many roommates prior to both of us had done the same there really made my stomach churn. About noon the first day, the doc still had not come in to see me, or had not called for me, and I was pissed. I wanted my regular clothes, not the damn prison garb, and I wanted to be on my way. All of a sudden, this medium sized black kid, probably no older than twenty, bellowed in a voice not of this world, and spoke damnations against the system and the pawns that enforced its rules, and said they would all burn, and he looked possessed when they took him down onto his bum and straitjacketed him away to reconditioning. Pretty traumatic stuff. Eventually, a nurse came for me; I had a visitor.

I went to the kitchen area, past the open-view windows of the nurses' base and on the other side of the gathering room where the television blared some news about the problem with the Los Angeles County sewer system. What do you have it, it was Dohltrey.

He took off his cap and brushed his hair back in a dramatic slow motion and put his head down when he sat across from me. I gathered he could not have been in a good mood from seeing me there. I didn't do him any favors to make me seem empathic, but he still acted as if he was. It bothered me. I had too much pride. I said, give it to me straight, no sugar or cherries on top. Why was he here? He waited and handed me some chocolate, figured I could use it. I chomped away. I got up and stared at the windows to the outside sun through the windows farthest on the other side of the TV room, through the windows on the nearest side of that room, and through the windows where the kitchen room was. And I felt layered in by so much lack of privacy. I turned back, and as I did, the camera at the corner of the room moved with me, so I believed, but I spit away what I had gathered in my thoughts with lack of concern for anyone else who could be hearing.

I figured he was the delegate, the one playing off both sides without being suspected by either one, and that the way it had come to now, if I was going to be placing blame because I wanted to, he had to have made out with Brubaker, and Dynamo was subject to his disposal whenever that could be useful. He denied the last claim, and said, they expect him to make forays into violating their code of fiduciary duty, that it was natural, in his self interests, and not necessarily damaging to their objectives. He said I had two options, but he knew I'd only really have one because only one made sense so he just told me that one after I pushed him to. It was to bide my time in here, or a rehabilitation facility, privately paid, which I knew of, and in exchange, any investigation that could potentially be pending in a matter of days or weeks would never come to pass; thus, I'd keep my money and keep my freedom as long as I took my own freedom away willfully for a month or two. It was an immediate answer he got, yes, because it was surely worth my time to keep the earnings for a job well executed, well, actually, seen through to the end, rather than hinge my future on a possible foray into the movie business. He ignored my logic and said once the time comes, sign on as voluntary, and a representative sent by him would initiate my transfer to a swanky rehab, in Malibu, I surely deserved that. He said some of it would come out of my pocket, then, and I said not a bother, it'd be a wash for all the dirt I'd come by to earn off the street, anyhow. He still felt bad and handed me an electronic cigarette, said he wished he could do more, that it wasn't personal, only business, whatever. The play was going and I'd be rid of this trouble if I was just meditative for the time being. Drug free, alcohol free, that was my punishment.

18

WHEN I got transferred, the day after I signed the papers after Dohltrey had told me to, I got a visit from Ollie Breeze. He considered Promises a place to have fun, that I should cavort with some celebutante types in residence, and that if he could pay for some retreat like this, it would not be such a bad thing. Like an adult summer camp, with rules like parents. At least they let me smoke here, and I chained away while we continued his mantra for rehabilitation on the terrace we were at overlooking the Malibu waves.

When he was spewing his idiosyncratic innocent bullshit, like it was all a show for his own pleasure, I considered how a place like this was a dilemma in practice. No one was ever going to get sober after the fact here, no one was going to come to appreciate what it's like to be free in America, because nothing on the surface was denied at such a place. It was as he had said, adult summer camp, with minimal restrictions, and if you were connected—which you had to be to get a space in a place like this—you could have all material amenities delivered at your command.

The charade still made me bitter though, because I could see it for what it was. If I had a sliver of faith that something could come out of such an arrangement, I'd have been better off. But I wasn't. When Breeze finished, he exclaimed that Rex was overcome with simultaneous grief and joy that I had been subjected to such uncomfortable treatment. But the silver lining was why he was joyous and that such an experience could make me a more substantive presence in his circle, and perhaps increase the likelihood that the script could have legs and told Ollie to make arrangements to work on the development of the story at my company on a daily basis. I was stuck with him, and this is where I began to reveal things that had truly transpired to get me where I was, and he was fascinated. Said this was gold. And with my permission, we could mesh storylines together, art on fiction, fiction on art, life as art, art as life. I really wished he had gotten rid of the clichéd axioms of imagination and just bare bones-ed it to the written word. After a few days though, he brought some personal goodies from Rex, including sunflower seeds, gummy worms, and a few books I actually wanted to read and reread. They could only be from someone who knew me at an utmost personal level, and it was probably Vittoria, but I didn't ask. Just was grateful for things I liked.

Within a month, we had worked like mad dogs and the development was good because it kept me occupied. A younger, smaller, more bubbly version of Vittoria with the same occupation had offered me some drugs and I passed, 'cause that wasn't my endgame at the time. A break couldn't be a bad thing.

Anyway, Ollie gave me grass for the work together and some leftovers in case I felt like smoking before bed. When it was getting close to the end of my stint, they said I could go out as long as I came back by a certain time and checked in, like at a halfway house. But I denied the desire and wanted to get out, I'd stay out when the time came. It came in two more weeks, and I didn't ask anyone to pick me up. Instead, I took a cab to Satch's and it was quiet, 4:30 on a workday and overcast cold so Los Angelenos stayed inside. I took notice of the place because I was so overcome with relief at my freedom at last.

Bright, sparkling items on the cherry wood counter, the lights coming from the emptying glasses and the empty ones behind the counter, the kaleidoscope of everything in the metal canister holding the remains of more malt for my shake, and the glistening white that could never get dirty of the boy behind the counter's uniform. Against all the red inside, the streetlights began to come on outside, and the sidewalk looked pale green, almost yellow, but not quite.

My friends knew it was my release date so my phone kept going off. I stepped out for a cigarette and to take Harley's call, because she was most adamant about getting my attention, calling and calling ceaselessly, and I asked her to be a doll, use my spare key that the superintendent had, and pick me up in my ride. Forty minutes or so later, she was there, and it was sweet because the car was off, parked right out front, and she had turned the lights on, so they crashed with the streetlights, and she was already in the passenger seat smoking when I came outside.

Our eyes met and didn't stay for I let her watch me cross the front, get in, rev the engine to life, and spark my own.

We sailed and rode on the concrete waves, taking it down Sunset to the Pacific Coast and picked up a bottle but let it slide beneath the backseats. We shared a joint and kept the music off, preferring the breeze from the tide and the full moon coming into plain view. We hit a high watermark on the road when it got dark, dark, where the lights of the cars behind disappeared for more than a moment, even though I knew they were still there, riding toward us, and I gunned the car to triple digits and broke free so when the headlights showed up again, they were more distinct and farther away than before.

And it wasn't even late, but there was only one car approaching from the opposite way and the red light called for both of us to stop, but as if we were reading each other's minds, in unison, we ran it on the same dare at the same time. The lights behind were long gone, and it felt good, like a good time to live. Along way away down that silent road.

THE END

9 781944 527006